DOGMA

DOGMA

··

Lars Iyer

 MELVILLE HOUSE
BROOKLYN, NEW YORK

DOGMA

Copyright © 2011 by Lars Iyer

First Melville House Printing: January 2012

Melville House Publishing
145 Plymouth Street
Brooklyn, New York 11201
mhpbooks.com

ISBN: 978-1-61219-046-4

Printed in the United States of America

1 2 3 4 5 6 7 8 9 10

Library of Congress Cataloging-in-Publication Data

Iyer, Lars.
Dogma / Lars Iyer.
    pages cm
ISBN 978-1-61219-046-4 (pbk.)
1. Philosophy--Fiction. I. Title.
PR6109.Y47D64 2011
823'.92--dc23
            2011045059

You should never learn from your mistakes, W. says. He never has, he says, which is why he associates with me. And nor have I learned from my mistakes, in all the years of our collaboration. Because I am incapable of learning.

Table manners, the art of conversation: what hasn't he tried to teach me? But I have barely learnt to keep my trousers on, W. says. I have barely learnt to sip my tea.

Even today, as we walk through the gorse towards the shore, he feels as though he's taking a lunatic out on day release, W. says. Listing my shortcomings above the sound of the breakers, he knows I've already forgotten everything he's said.

The roaring of the sea is like the roaring of my stupidity, W. says. It's a terrible sound, but a magnificent one, too. It's the sound of *un*learning, he says. It's *the sound of Lars*, of the chaos that undoes every idea.

My stupidity: that's what saves him, W. says. If it weren't for my stupidity, where would he be? He wouldn't have learnt the fundamental lesson, W. says. He wouldn't have understood that the great tasks of thought must begin from a kind of *non*-thought, that achievement — real achievement — is only possible once you've passed through the most abject of failures.

What would Socrates have been, without knowing that he knew nothing? What would Nicholas of Cusa have been, without his *learned ignorance*?

Isn't that why he's kept me close?, W. says. Isn't that why he's refused to learn from his biggest mistake?

W. has no great love of nature, he says as we walk. The sublimity of nature, mountain peaks, the surging ocean, all that: it means nothing to him. He's a man of the city, W. says. And if we're out of the city today — *apolis*, as the Greeks would say — it is only to return to the city refreshed, catching the bus back from Cawsand to Plymouth.

His city, W. says. But not for much longer. By what cruel fate will he be made to leave? For what reason will he be *forced out*? He knows the time will come. He's always known it, which has made his relationship to the city that much more intense. He's always known the city would *slip through his fingers*.

Anyway, he's glad to be out of the college for the day, W. says, as the path rises into Cawsand. He's glad I've flown in from the north. There are rumours in the corridors, he says. There are murmurings in the quadrangle. Compulsory redundancies . . . the restructuring of the college . . . the closure of whole departments, whole faculties . . . It's a bit like ancient Rome, before they stabbed Caesar to death, W. says.

Of course, he'll have to leave if he loses his job, W. says. He'll have to take to the roads. Because there's no work here, not in Plymouth, he says.

And won't it be the same for me? Won't I eventually be driven out of my city? —'Don't think you're safe', W. says. 'Don't think you're going to live out your life in the pubs of Newcastle'.

'They're coming to get us', W. says. Who? Who's coming?, I ask him. He's not sure. But somewhere, far away, our fate has already been decided.

The end is coming, W. says, he's sure of that. Our end, or the end of the world? —'Both!', W. says. The one is inseparable from the other. Do I see it as he does? Is he the only one who can see the signs?

He sees them even now, on this sunny day in Cawsand. He sees them in our honey beer, W. says. In the dog that drops a stone at my feet, wanting me to play with it. In the narrowness of the three-storeyed house opposite. In the name of the pub where we are drinking: *The Rising Sun*. And in me, too? —'In you above all', W. says.

But what sun will rise over us?, W. asks, as he drains his second pint. A black sun, he says. A sun of ashes and darkness. He sees the image in his mind's eye: the man and boy of

The Road, pushing a shopping cart down an empty highway. Only, in our case, it'll be two men, squabbling over whose turn it is to ride in the cart. Two men with ashes in their hair, exiled from their cities and from all cities.

At the bus stop, W. tells me about his current intellectual projects. They can be summed up under the general heading, *capitalism and religion*, he says. The 'and' is designed to be provocative, W. says. He wants to provoke the *new atheists*, he says. There's nothing more infuriating than the *new atheists*.

Of course, by religion, W. means Judaism. And by Judaism, he means the Judaism of Cohen and Rosenzweig. If only the new atheists could read Rosenzweig and Cohen, W. says. If only *he* could read, really read, Rosenzweig and Cohen, he says.

And by capitalism? Our world, W. says. Our whole lives . . . Hasn't capitalism entered a new phase?, W. says. Hasn't it entered every particle, element and moment of our lives?

Capitalism *and* religion . . . He'd appreciate my input as a Hindu, W. says, as the bus arrives. What would a Hindu make of all this?, he wonders. But he knows I have no answer.

My Hinduism has no *depth*, W. says. He can't believe in it, not really. —'Convince me', he says. 'Convince me you're a Hindu. In what does your Hinduism consist?'

I come from a long line of Hindus, he knows that, W.

says. Generations of Brahmin priests, performing rites and ceremonies! Generations of descendants of the great sages, full of sacred knowledge, trained in reading the holy scriptures.

But what do I actually *know* about Hinduism?, W. wonders. If he drew a Venn diagram with the set *Hinduism* and the set *Lars*, where would they intersect?

But *capitalism*, now, W. says, as we find our seats. There I might know something. Didn't I come into contact with the *essence of capitalism* during my long periods of warehouse work and unemployment? Didn't I learn what it was really about, as I stapled gaudy pictures of Hindu gods to the walls of my work cubicle?

W. has always been in awe of my *years in the world*, as he calls them. —'How did you survive out there?' I barely survived, of course, W. says. I nearly didn't survive . . . But that makes my experiences even more valuable, W. says.

Capitalism and religion, W. says. Or, in my case, *failed* capitalism and *failed* religion. Somehow, I'm the key to his project, W. says. Somehow I'm the key to the copula, though he's not sure how.

At Whitsand, the bus stops to let on some of the famous *Poles of Plymouth*. There are hundreds of them working in the bars and cafés, W. says. Thousands of Poles with shining faces! They've brought grace to his city, he says. Grace and refinement.

W. muses upon the troubled history of Poland — how,

over centuries, the borders of the country have moved outward and inward like a concertina, accompanying the melancholy music of war, genocide and occupation, the great lament of Old Europe. He hears it still, W. says. It sounds through his blood. Didn't his father's family come to England, generations ago, because of old European pogroms? Isn't W., too, a Polish immigrant?

As we stretch our legs on the ferry to Devonport, we remember the Polish waitress who served us at W.'s favourite café. How gentle she was! How *generous*! She had everything we lacked, he says. A delicate intelligence . . . Wit . . . Poise . . . I was moved, W. says, he could see that. I blushed. I fumbled for words.

I should find myself a Plymouth Pole, W. says. That might be my path to redemption. But even a Plymouth Pole would need to be courted, W. says.

You have to *court* women, W. says. You can't just jump into bed with them. He courted Sal for eight months, he says. He plied her with gin, and she burned CDs for him. Those were the best of times, W. says. The uncertainty. The intoxication. They were drunk six nights out of seven.

But what would I know of all that? There's no tenderness in me, W. says. Lust, yes. A kind of animal craving. Foam on the lips. I'm like one of those monkeys in the zoo with an inflamed arse—what are they called? Oh yes, *mandrills*. I'm the mandrill of romance, W. says.

'Watch!', says W. It's the famous sequence of the chicken dancing in an amusement arcade booth, from Herzog's film *Stroszek*. Bruno, the film's protagonist, puts a few quarters in the slot and wanders off to shoot himself. The chicken dances, bobbing on its claws. The chicken dances, its comb wobbling, its wattle swinging, its black eyes manic . . .

Bruno and the others have come to America to escape the old world. They've come to escape the past! And what does Bruno find? The dancing chicken, W. says.

Herzog speaks of finding images adequate to the world, to the state of the world, W. says. —'The chicken is one of those images, don't you see?' I see.

Stroszek: didn't Ian Curtis watch the film just before he killed himself? He saw the chicken, W. says. He *really* saw it, and it was too much for him. Perhaps it'll be the same with us. Perhaps America will be too much for us.

Ah, why do we get invited on these lecture tours?, W. says. What do people expect? In truth, we should refuse all invitations. We shouldn't go anywhere! Isn't Bruno's fate a warning to us all, that we should go *nowhere near America*?

The chicken is cosmic, that's what we have to understand,

W. says. It's a bit like that statue I have in my flat. Who is it supposed to be again? Lord Shiva as Nataraja, I tell him. The cosmic dancer. Ah yes, he remembers, W. says. The dance of the cosmos, the cosmos as a dance, all that sort of thing.

'What's your cosmic dance like?', W. asks. 'It's the funky chicken, isn't it? Go on, fat boy. Dance'.

W. likes to watch me dance, he says. It's so improbable. So graceless. W. admires my *non-dancing*, as he calls it. I am a non-dancer, he says. But the '*non-*' of my non-dancing is not privative, that's the secret, he says. It's liberatory! I'm not like the others, who only dance in their chains. I'm not a *victim of choreography*.

Of course, I'm also a *non-thinker*, W. says, which is in no way liberatory. —'You *seem* to think. You *look like* you're thinking, but in fact you're doing nothing of the sort'. He grants that I *feel* a great deal—I am subject to great waves of pathos—but that's not the same as thinking. 'You're a *pathetic* man, but not a *thinking* man', W. says.

Still, W. suspects that the power of thinking—*his* thinking—might be joined to my non-thinking. Might the attempt to think *messianism*, the current stage of W.'s *Denkweg*, his thought-path, require a kind of *pathos*? Perhaps there's something like a messianic *mood*, W. muses.

The chicken won't stop. That's what's etched into the runoff groove of the last Joy Division album. *The chicken won't stop*: it's like a mantra to W. —'You won't stop, will you?', he says. That's part of the horror: I show no signs of stopping. But it's part of my glory, too. Who am I amusing? Not even him. And certainly not anyone else.

Innocence . . . artlessness . . . a kind of childlike simplicity . . . In my best moments, I really do resemble Bruno Stroszek, W. says. In my *best* moments, he emphasises. Otherwise I resemble no one but myself, more's the pity.

But sometimes I achieve a kind of *pathetic grandeur*, W. says, almost despite myself. There I sit, in the squalor. There I am, a squalid man amidst the squalor, beer cans and discounted sandwich boxes lying empty around me, plaster dust in my hair, and I say something truly striking. I make some pronouncement. —'You're like a savant', W. says.

If I resemble Bruno Stroszek, W. supposes that he can only resemble Bruno's elderly neighbour —'what was his name? Scheitzer? Scheitzerhund?' Just Scheitz, I tell him, Mr Scheitz. Mr Scheitz had an interest in *animal magnetism*, W. remembers. He bothered people with it. He confused them. That's how it is with *his* interests, W. says, which are equally improbable, equally irrelevant.

Heathrow. W. has a horror of airports, he says. Herded through corridors! Driven, like cattle in a slaughterhouse! You can smell the panic, W. says.

Krasznahorkai writes about the horror of airports, W. says. About the way they need all of your concentration. Every bit of it. About the dreadful din, the chaos, the constant flow of people. About the stony-faced guards, hands on their machine guns, looking in thirty-six directions at once.

We mustn't joke in the security queues, W. says. We mustn't laugh, or they'll beat us with their rubber truncheons. They blind us with tear gas and then they'll gun us down, like dogs.

But I'm at home in an airport, he can see that. I like the fear. I like being driven, herded, forced along. It's because I'm fundamentally *bureaucratic*, W. says. I'm an *administrator of the spirit*.

Even an administrator of the spirit can get it wrong, W. says when we arrive in Nashville airport in the early hours. Have I really lost our hosts' address? Will we really have to wait until morning to contact the university for their phone number? There's nothing for it but to pass the night on the rocking chairs in the airport lounge.

W. takes his copy of Spinoza's *Ethics* from his man bag, the only thing you can do at times like this. —'Spinoza teaches you to affirm everything', W. says. 'Affirm, affirm, affirm, that's what Spinoza says'. But W. can't affirm the copy of *National Enquirer* I buy at the kiosk, nor the Twinkies I stuff into my mouth. Somehow I always stand in the way of his beatitude.

This is a *car city*, W. notices of Nashville, as we are shown the sights. —'You're nothing without a car!'

They tried to do without one when they first arrived in America, our Canadian hosts tell us. They cycled everywhere, for miles and miles. People cried out to them in the streets. —'Why are you cycling? Are you crazy?' But our hosts continued to cycle. They cycled out to their favourite Mexican restaurant and their favourite Vietnamese restaurant. And in the end it was too much.

Our hosts have been forced into driving, they tell us, which is terrible. No one should be forced to drive, W. says. Especially not Canadians! The Canadian, in his imagination, paddles canoes through the wilderness. The Canadian rides horses! The Canadian sleds across the pristine snow! The Canadian is not made to be a driver.

He should know, W. says. He spent his childhood in Canada. Didn't he paddle his canoe on the lakes of Canada? Didn't he ride a horse through the Canadian forests? That's why he's never learnt to drive, W. says: to stay loyal to his Canadian childhood.

Downtown Nashville consists largely of car parks. Odd bits

of metal stick out of the ground at shin height. There's no one around except a fully outfitted cowboy walking down the street. —'Must be German', W. says.

Where, we wonder, are the *people* of Nashville? That's one thing we like about our cities, we agree: there are always people about. They're usually drunk, of course. Drunk and lairy. But that is a good sign.

We visit the full-sized concrete replica of the Parthenon, which sits vast and unapologetic in the sun. Nashville's supposed to be the *Athens of the South*, our hosts tell us. The Athens of the South! I should feel at home here with my formidable knowledge of ancient languages, W. says.

W. insists on buying us souvenir togas. I take a picture of us posing on the steps. W. feels like Socrates, he says. And I am Diogenes, Socrates's idiot double, a man who looked exactly like him, but who begged for a living, and lived in a barrel in the marketplace, his shameless habits scandalising all of Athens.

Of course, Diogenes merely *acted* like an idiot, W. says. He lived in squalor, true enough—but that was because he despised the conventions of society. He lived in poverty—but that was because of a disdain for the stupidity of the rich. He was shameless—but that was because he thought human beings lived artificially and hypocritically.

Diogenes had a terrible wisdom of his own, even Plato granted that, W. says. He had a terrible philosophy, which he taught by living example. A *Socrates gone mad*, that's what

Plato called him. A *Socrates*, because Diogenes, too, believed in reason, exalting it above custom and tradition. But a Socrates *gone mad*, because Diogenes took shamelessness to a new extreme: eschewing all modesty, pissing on people who insulted him, shitting in the theatre and masturbating in the public square . . .

A *Diogenes gone mad*, W. says: that's how he thinks of me. A man without shame, not because he rejects ideas of human decency but because he knows no better. A man outside of society, not because he was an ascetic but because no one wanted him in it.

W. insists on being shown *old* Nashville, although there's very little of it left. Our hosts take us to Nashville City Cemetery, and I take pictures of the old gravestones. They drive us by the old McCann grocery, just off Broadway, and I photograph the skyscrapers reflected in its windows. But W.'s looking for something else, he says. He can't explain exactly what.

W. tells me to photograph the words *closeing sale* graffitied across a shuttered shopfront. He tells me to photograph the rusting stairwells and broken glass in the derelict brewery, and the poster advertising *free Ninja lessons* stapled on a telegraph pole.

W. tells me to take a photo of an abandoned roller skating rink, and of a closed up loading bay. He tells me to photograph a sofa stranded on the sidewalk, and the neon signs on several Mexican restaurants (*Los Happy Bellies, Los Hipopótamos . . .*) Then he directs me to take a picture of the view of the sky through the girders of the pedestrian bridge that leads downtown.

W. speaks of *kernels of time*, and *dialectical images*. He speaks of *re-enchantment* and *re-awakening*. He speaks of the *tradition of the oppressed . . .*

W.'s looking for the *America hidden by America*, he says. The *submerged America* of the poor, W. says: that's part of it, he says. The *third world America* of the wretched and the broken-hearted, he says. But also, close by, as hope is always close to despair, a *messianic America*; an America re-enchanted and re-awakening; a perpetually new America stretching its limbs in the sun . . .

At *Katie K.'s Prairie Style*, W. decides to be my dresser. He knows I've always wanted a Nudie Suit, or at the very least a Western-style shirt. I want embroidery! I want fringes!

W. fetches me Western-style shirts, bolo ties and cowboy boots, while I stand in the dressing room in my underpants. But nothing works. I still don't look like a Rhinestone Cowboy.

Over lunch, our hosts tell us of their *Nashville misery*. W. does impressions of me to cheer them up. —'This is Lars thinking', he says, making chimp noises. 'This is Lars speaking German', he says, making louder chimp noises. 'This is Lars reading Rosenzweig', he says, falling silent and scratching his head. But our hosts are unmoved. They're too full of *American despair*.

W. takes me aside before we get back in the car. I should talk more, W. says. I should try and engage with our hosts!

Ah, why have I never learnt to talk?, he wonders. Why has it always been left to him, when we're in company, to speak for both of us? For long periods, I'm mute, thinking of God knows what, W. says. I'm like some great block of stupidity. Like some great stupid Easter Island statue . . .

What does stupidity think about?, W. wonders. Is it ever aware of its own stupidity? Does it scratch its head and wonder about itself? Ah, but stupidity can never uncover its own truth, that's its tragedy, W. says. Stupidity can never look itself in the face.

Sometimes he likes my silence, W. says. He imagines it to be a kind of integrity—a way of guarding something, some secret. 'He knows something', W. says to himself, looking across at me. Or, better: 'something knows itself in him'.

One day, they'll decrypt me, W. likes to think to himself. One day, the Rosetta Stone of my stupidity will yield up its secrets. —'You see!', W. will say. 'I told you so!', he'll say, when they solve my riddle.

Perhaps we should be silent about fundamental matters, W. says. Perhaps there's nothing we can say that does not immediately destroy what is most important.

But there's silence and silence, W. says . . . There is the reserve of the wise man, full of learning, full of modesty, who knows that the truth is infinitely subtle, infinitely complex, and that one must never speak too soon. And there is the roaring silence of the idiot, W. says, which resounds with dark matter and barren wastes and bacteria — with everything that is unredeemed in the universe.

Americans don't go in for gardening, we notice as we near our hosts' street: the back garden — brown grass, uncut — simply runs out unfenced onto the road behind. It's exactly the same with the front garden. But Americans are tremendously neighbourly. Didn't our hosts' neighbour bake a pie for us, when she heard we were coming to stay?

Hospitality is a great sign of civilisation, W. says. Our houses should be wholly open to our guests. The guest turns the house into an offering . . . Of course, I have a flat, not a house, but the same thing holds. And my flat has little to offer except squalor and damp, but the same principle applies.

How many guests W. has welcomed! How many great minds have crossed his threshold! He's opened his drinks cabinet to them, and his enormous fridge. He's opened every kitchen cupboard, to whip up a midnight snack for some great mind or other. He's had whole *parties* of guests, each person staying in another of his many rooms, each for whom W. threw open his airing cupboard anew, for fresh sheets and fresh duvet covers. Fresh towels!

How many times has he projected *Stroszek* for his guests on the walls of his vast living room? How many times has he *danced in his socks* with them to apocalyptic Canadian pop?

And what about me? Who have I had to stay? What thinkers have passed through my door? Just him, W. says. Just him, breathing in mould spores and plaster dust. Just him, wondering why the lights don't work and the TV doesn't work and the fridge doesn't work and why the oven is upside down in the living room.

On the porch, with our *sipping gin*. Joggers and dog-walkers fill the streets. Fireflies hover over the grasses. This is what they should drink, here in the South, W. says: Plymouth Gin, neat, over ice.

Capitalism and religion, W. muses. Capitalism *and* religion. —'You never were religious', W. says. I'm a Hindu!, I tell him. 'But you were never *really* religious, were you?'

My Hinduism seems all too easy to W. It brings me no anxiety. It fails to push me further. I don't struggle with my faith, or with the idea of God.

W.'s relation to religion is fraught, he says. It's a daily struggle. Sometimes he feels on the brink of a great conversion, to what he doesn't quite know. But at other times he feels as far from religion as could be, and the word *faith* is ashes in his mouth.

Of course, W. was born a Jew — he's Jewish through his father's line, but his mother's family were Catholic converts, and he was baptised. He went through a great religious phase at the age of nine!, W. remembers. He demanded to be taken to church. And he was taken, although his family were lapsed. —'Nine!', W. says. That's when he was most pious, W. says. Most pure.

Our hosts' CD collection. The Golden Gate Quartet, Barbeque Bob, The Hokum Boys, The Mississippi Sheiks: who are these people? Our hosts are opting out of contemporary life, W. says. They're in internal exile. They're ransacking the past — a never-existing, arcadian past — to save themselves in the present.

W. puts on the Mississippi Sheiks. You pronounce it *sheeks*, apparently, he says, reading the inlay. W. admires the sophisticated harmonies, and the subtle interplay of instruments. It's about rhythm, he says, not about melody. W.'s becoming an enemy of melody, he says. He hates *dead syncopations*. He hates *drums*.

But what would any of this mean to me? I'm a Jandek fanatic, for fuck's sake! He does an impression of Jandek's singing. —'*I'm in paaaaaainn*'; '*No one liiiiikes me*'. Actually, he respects Jandek, W. says. My instincts were right, for once. We tried to have a *Jandek party*, of course, down in W.'s house. We forced his students and Sal to sit and listen in silence. —'How long could they stand it?', W. asks. 'How long?' He pauses dramatically. '*Three seconds!*', he says. 'That's all they could take. I think Sal shat herself', he says. She's never forgiven us for that.

W. laments that I'm no longer open, really open, to music. —'You only listen to Jandek', he says. It's quite impressive. W. has a certain respect for my obsessions, although they're absurdly narrowing. My whole life has been nothing other than a series of obsessions, W. says, and this is my latest one.

There's no point in putting any books in his man bag for our trips, W. says, because he is soon too drunk to read. And there's no point in carrying his notebook either, because he is soon too drunk to think.

How long have we been away? Two days? Three? But W.'s beginning to forget his former life. Hasn't he always lived in this way, wandering around America with a moron?

Ah, why did he bring me to America?, W. wonders. What is it, in him, that desires his destruction? There'd be sense in bringing someone along to inspire him, W. says, but not to destroy him. Unless it's his death-drive, W. says. Unless *I'm* his death-drive, for how else can he account for it?

Sometimes, W. thinks that I'm like those people Russell Crowe sees, in *A Beautiful Mind*. A hallucination. A figment of his imagination. But I'm real, quite real, that's the trouble. You can exorcise a ghost. But how can you rid yourself of an idiot?

My own corner, that's where I should stay, W. says. *My own corner*, with my own interests, which are contracting by the day . . . But W. insists on bringing me into the world, doesn't he? Why?, he wonders. For what reason?

He had a terrible dream last night, W. says. I was leading him up one of the hills outside Nashville, grim faced and silent. I was much larger than usual, a giant toad, a giant flea with great thick thighs. And W. was much smaller, a wren, a midge. And I was silent: I wasn't saying a word. I was dragging him up the hill without offering a word of explanation.

'Tell me, tell me where we're going!', W. cried. But I would tell him nothing. On the hill summit, late evening, W. found himself prone, and I had a knife to his throat. I was silent. I was about to cut . . . W. waited for a voice telling me to stop. He waited for God to intervene, telling me to sacrifice something else in W.'s place. But no voice came.

W.'s dream. It must have been because I was talking about Hindu sacrifice the other night, W. says. About the four hundred kinds of sacrifice detailed in the Vedas. About the *macrocosm*, about *cosmogony* and *anthropogony*.

When the priest pours the offering into the fire — milk or ghee, vegetable cakes or the stalks of the soma plant — he is communicating with the divine realm, I told him. The fire itself is divine, I told him. Destruction itself is godly.

W. shudders. That's why I'm destroying myself, isn't it? That's why I'm setting myself on fire. It's part of some mad Hindu scheme. My life, the disaster of my career, is only *a spoonful of ghee for the fire*.

But there's worse, W. says. He's going to be sacrificed, too. His life, his thought, the disaster of his career will be just another offering for the flames.

Our hosts don't understand our bickering, W. says. It upsets them. Don't they see that it's the only way we can express affection? It's a British working class thing, W. told them, but they only looked at us blankly.

We've become strange, W. says. We've spent too much time in each other's company. Even Sal can't save us from that. We're no longer fit for human society, W. says. For *Canadian* society.

How long will it be before our hosts turn us out onto the streets?, W. wonders. We've sinned against their hospitality. We've desecrated their home. Our bickering (*my* bickering) . . . Our hysteria (*my* hysteria) . . . Our sense of living in a perpetual emergency (*my* sense of living in a perpetual emergency).

I'm a disgrace, W. says. My table manners! My habit of continually scratching myself. —'And why are you always touching your chest through your shirt?', he says.

Isn't it bad enough that our hosts are imprisoned in Nashville?, W. says. Haven't they got enough to deal with? The British working class guest is an unruly guest, W. says. It's been up to him, W., to maintain a certain standard of behaviour. But I always let him down, don't I? I always drag him into the mire.

Capitalism is the *evil twin* of true religion, said W. in our Nashville presentation. Capitalism is a kind of cult, he said. It's the mysterious force that sustains our lives. And money is the false God we worship.

Schuld: the German word for *guilt* also means debt, W. explained. Capitalism functions on credit, so we are all guilty.

Consume!, that's the commandment of capitalism, W. told our audience. It sustains the fantasy that the repayment of debt can be endlessly postponed, he said. Hidden by this fantasy is *real material destruction*, he said, which makes limitless debt possible in the short term and impossible over the longer term.

When we were asked what we meant by *real material destruction*, W. pointed to me. —'Look at him!' The audience laughed. 'No, really, look at him!', W. said.

W. was going to tell them about the end of the world, he says. He was going to tell them about the *real* apocalypse. And he was going to tell them about messianism, too — about *true* religion, which neither the capitalist nor the new atheist will ever understand.

But our audience looked bored, yawning and fidgetting. —'Six people', W. says. 'Six bored people, looking at their watches. Did we come all this way for that?'

Jake's Bar, Five Points. W. berates the bartender for the poor range of gin. —'Bombay Gin is terrible', he tells her. 'Tanqueray isn't bad, especially with tonic, but Bombay Gin is a marketing gimmick'.

Her customers like it, she says. W. tells her to introduce them to Plymouth Gin. —'Why haven't you got any Plymouth Gin? You can get it in America'. Our bartender looks annoyed. She'll get what her customers want, she says. —'But how do they know what they want when they haven't tried Plymouth Gin?', W. says.

W.'s *flying blind* in America, he says to me. He is not understood over here. W.'s used to explaining *me* to people, but not having to explain himself. He's a *force for good*—can't people see that?

Anyway, it's another sign of the *step change in capitalism*, when Plymouth Gin is taken to be a gin like any other, W. says. It's a sign of the end, he says, when you can no longer make *real distinctions*.

At night, our open-hearted hosts dream of the Yukon, W.'s sure of that. The mountains, the open spaces . . . the fawn-like gentleness of the Yukonites . . . the lakes, beside which you can pitch your tepee: I can't imagine it, W. says. Back home, our hosts probably spent whole summers by the Yukon lakes in their teepees.

Canadians are people of the expanses, W. says. They have expansive souls. They come into their own out of doors, taking great strides in the wilderness. They're only really themselves when they go horse riding or kayaking, W. says, and when singing close harmonies around the fire at night.

W. speaks of the Canadian summer, of days that go on forever, and of the Canadian autumn, when the aurora borealis flashes out above the frosts. And he speaks of the Canadian winter, when your breath freezes in the air and the absolute clarity of the Milky Way crowns you with stars, pin-prick sharp in the frozen sky.

The Canadian is a friend of the bear, and of the wolf, W. explains. The Canadian is a friend of his fellow Canadian *by way* of his friendship with the bear and the wolf. The wilderness opens between them, Canadians. They safeguard it; they inhale it and they exhale it; it's the element of their lives, W. says.

It was the element of his life, too, he says, before his family returned from Canada. Ah, his Canadian years! He knows something of teepee life. He knows something of close harmonies sung in the Canadian night. But now, like me, he has trouble imagining himself in a teepee.

W.'s tried to explain England to our hosts. —'You can't imagine what it's like', he's said. He's spoken of tight corners and narrow corridors, of rats crawling over rats. He's spoken of class war, and of the triumph of *opportunism and cynicism.* —'Look at us!', he has cried. 'Look at him!', he has said, pointing to me. 'Can't you see?'

The *circle of my obsessions* has become narrower, W. says. That's the essential change he's seen over the years.

Once, they encompassed the whole world, my obsessions. I took them for ambition, genuine ambition. I wanted to learn things, master whole areas of knowledge. My God, I even took myself for a philosopher.

'You studied, didn't you? You read. You even *wrote*. You—wrote! It's amazing', W. says. 'You wrote and published'.

What temerity! What lack of understanding! Yes, I'd deluded myself completely, it was quite magnificent. I'd taken myself for a scholar, a man of letters. I wrote learned articles. I spoke with learned people on learned topics . . .

I thought I was part of something, didn't I? —I walked in cloisters, in Oxford colleges, with my hands behind my back and my chin tilted upwards. My voice resounded beneath the vaulted ceilings. Ambition—that's what I thought I had, isn't it?

Everyone laughed. —'We were all laughing up our sleeves, but you didn't notice, did you?' The *circle of my obsessions* had not closed tight around my neck. I wasn't yet being strangled. It wasn't yet a garrotte . . .

And then what happened? He saw it, W. says. He was there. My obsessions didn't range as freely. My horizons shrank. Once, philosophy and literature; once, the great ideas of Europe: and now? A squalid room in a squalid flat. A pile of Jandek CDs. A cheap bottle of wine . . .

It's growing tighter, isn't it, the circle of my obsessions?, W. says. Tighter, until it's begun to strangle me. Tighter, and now my face is turning blue. I'm gasping for breath, aren't I?

At the bus station, an armed policeman behind the counter watches us menacingly. What have we done? Something very wrong, we feel. There's something very wrong with us. —'With *you*', W. says.

Sal's keeping our tickets safe, which is the best thing, we agree. We're lucky to have her on our side. What would we do if it weren't for her? Who would see us safely onto the Greyhound? —'She's our eyes', says W. 'And our ears. And our sense'. We're idiots in America, W. says.

We think back to Herzog's film: W. is the elderly neighbour, Mr Scheitz, and I'm Bruno. Without Sal, America would overwhelm us. It'd be just like the film, W. says. Without Sal, we'd buy a rifle from somewhere, like the characters in the film, and go to rob a bank. The bank would be closed, of course, just like in *Stroszek*, and we'd rob the barber shop next door. Then we'd head across to the supermarket with our thirty-two dollars, to spend our loot.

Then what would happen? W. would be arrested, just as Mr Scheitz is arrested, and I would run into the amusement arcade, feeding quarters into the various stalls, to set the rabbit climbing up on his fire truck, the duck playing his bass drum, and the chicken dancing . . .

And then what? Then I would ride off on the ski-lift with my rifle, just like Bruno, and shoot myself in the head . . .

Our bus is delayed. —'It's always late', says the woman standing in front of us. She's heading to a funeral, several states away. —'Won't make it now', she says. There's no information anywhere about the delay. There's no information booth, no one to ask.

We're the only white people in the bus station. Why is that?, we ask the woman in front. Where are the students? Have they all got cars? Where are the *white* poor? —'They don't take the bus', she says. The policeman watches on resignedly, a holstered gun pulled up round his shoulder.

They don't take the bus: these words are like a blow to W. Just like the blow of realising that there is no train station in Nashville. A city without a train station!, W. says. He can barely imagine it. A city without trains!

On the big TV screen, they're showing a documentary on airplane crashes, with footage of one crash after another. Screeching brakes. Metal crunching. Screams.

W.'s becoming hysterical. —'Why don't they tell us anything?', he cries. 'Are we cattle?'

I sit him on the floor and tell him Hindu stories to calm him down. I tell him how Ganesha came to have the head of an elephant, and Daksha the head of a goat. I tell him of the sage who temporarily substituted a horse's head for his own, knowing that the secret wisdom he was about to gain would shatter it into a million pieces. ('That's what would happen to you if you ever had an idea', W. says.) And I tell him how Dadhyanc's head was lopped off for revealing the secret of the sacrifice to human beings.

'Hinduism is a bloody religion', W. says.

On the bus. W. opens his man bag to show me what he's brought to read on our trip to Memphis. Rosenzweig, of course. You need a volume of Rosenzweig with you at all times, W. says. Polyani's *The Great Transformation*. And Whitman's *Leaves of Grass*, which dreams of what America might have been, W. says.

We must read if we want to live, W. says. We may have forgotten how to live, but they—the authors of the books in his man bag—have not.

And what have I brought? —'Maimon's autobiography. Oh yes, very good. Scholem's memoir of Benjamin. Very impressive'. But he knows I won't open my books, W. says. He knows I've got a *National Enquirer* concealed somewhere on my person.

W. doesn't believe I actually read books. —'They're like totems to you', he says. 'They contain what you lack. You surround yourself with them, but you don't understand them'.

My office is filled with books, that's the paradox, W. says. I get a childlike excitement from them, from the *fact* of them, with their heady titles and colourful spines.

Of course, the real reader has no need to surround himself with books, W. says. The real reader lends them to others, without a thought of them being returned. What need has he for a library of books? He prefers to be alone with only the most essential works, like Beckett with his Dante, in his room at the old folks' home. Beckett with his Dante, and cricket on the TV.

Memphis, unexpectedly, is *cold*. The taxi driver tells us that the weather doesn't know what it's doing. We go to *Gap* to buy warm clothes. To *Gap*! In *Memphis*! Imagine! The last place we wanted to go!

Gap's impossibly cheap. How can clothes be so cheap? In what mess of exploitation have we been caught? But we're cold, we have to compromise.

I buy a hoodie, W. a cardigan. We examine ourselves in the full length mirror. We look *preppy*, we decide, without knowing what this word means. We look like *preppies*.

It's still cold outside. What are we going to do? We rent a pool table. Preppies play pool, we decide.

We're being followed, W. observes, and it's true. The same rough-looking guys we saw earlier are slumped in leather chairs in the pool hall.

They hate preppies and want to rid the world of them, W. says. Which is fine, because he thinks he hates preppies and wants to rid the world of them. They're going to beat us to death, and he'll welcome it. But we outlast our would-be assailants, who tire of watching us playing bad pool and drinking.

The word *barbeque* doesn't mean the same thing over here, says W. over dinner. Nor does the word *ribs*. He's right. What have we been served? Vast oval plates of red-cooked meat. French fries in great piles. It's frightening. I must be in heaven with my enormous greed, W. says. My life has peaked at this point, hasn't it? I've finally found a country where I don't feel perpetually starved to death.

W. has always liked chubby men, he says. We recall the fat singers we admire, who drink wine out of bottles on stage. Fat, angry men. Is he angry because he's fat?, I ask of the singer in Modest Mouse. —'No, he was angry and then he got fat', W. says. Do you think he *minds* being fat?, I ask. —'He has other issues', W. says.

Of course, Kafka was thin, W. reminds me. Yes, but he was ill. Blanchot was thin, too, says W. But he was ill as well. —'I bet Brod was fat'. Definitely, I agree. He drank too much, that's why he got fat. —'Why do you think he drank?', W. asks. Because he knew he wasn't Kafka, I tell him.

We watch a band on Beale Street playing for tips. There are preppies everywhere, all around us. W. hates them. What are we doing here?, he says. Between songs, the singer comes round the crowd with a hat.

People have to promote themselves in America, we've noticed that. They're not ashamed of it, as they would be back home. There's no welfare state, that's what does it, W. says. But playing for preppies! It's the ultimate indignity, W. says, over our pints of Big Ass Beer.

It's my birthday today, reads the sign on the windshield of the taxi carrying us home. We ask our driver to tell us about the old Beale Street, before it became a tourist trap. —'It was a rough place. People getting stabbed. *Pee Wee's . . . The Panama . . . The Hole in the Wall*. They're long gone', he says. 'The gambling houses, too. Even the pool rooms . . . Beale Street was torn down after Dr King was assassinated . . . They rebuilt it in the '80s for the tourists . . . '

He tells us about how he saw Howlin' Wolf play one of the bars of old Beale Street, back in the '50s. —'Wolf'd crawl around the stage on all fours, howling', he says. 'That's how he got his name. And then, 'Wolf'd get women to ride up on his back. And then he'd go round the crowd. He had an extra-long microphone cord, see. Sometimes he'd go out and sing in the street. He'd howl at the moon . . . ' He laughs.

'Is it really your birthday?', W. asks him. 'Every day's my birthday', he says.

In the hotel bar, W. muses on our lecture tour. It's not going well, is it?, he says. It's going badly, I agree. Worse than ever. But why does it surprise us?, W. wonders. What did we expect? Some Kant-like resurgence, late in life? Some late awakening from our dogmatic slumbers?

Our presentations are so *polite*, he says. So conventional. We should learn from Howlin' Wolf, he says. We need more *pathos* in our presentations. More *fire*. We need to *howl at the moon* . . .

Isn't that what W. has always hoped to hear in our

presentations: my howling at the moon? The great cry of non-thinking: isn't that what he's waiting for? But all I've ever managed is the *mewling of the imbecile*, W. says.

Ah, when will we learn how to speak like *real* philosophers?, W. says. When will philosophy itself sing through our presentations?

Philosophy itself. W. imagines us like the Delphic Pythia, speaking for the Oracle, interpreting what it said. He imagines us like the hierophants of the Eleusian Mysteries, bringing congregants into the presence of the holy.

Philosophy *itself* would speak, W. says, and we would interpret what it said for our audiences. Philosophy itself would sound through our presentations, like the wind through a wind harp.

He's too scholarly, W. says. Too concerned with footnotes and references, and appeals to the great names of philosophy. And as for me . . . W. shakes his head. What can he say? It's not simply that I'm *un*scholarly, that I haven't mastered the protocols, which of course I haven't. It's more than that, W. says. I'm *non*-scholarly, W. says, where the '*non-*' means much more than a simple negation.

I'm a parody of the scholar: of course. I'm a grotesque double of the real philosopher: very true. But it's more than that . . . *I pay no heed to philosophy whatsoever*, W. says. Reason, rigorous argument: none of it means anything to me. In its way, it's admirable, W. says. But the effect on my audiences has been terrible.

My booming. My near-bellowing . . . W., as my co-presenter, has to sit beside me as I babble. W. has to field questions for me, and explain me to our fellow conference-goers.

Ostracism, that's what I've brought him, W. says. Derision. Every door that was open to him is now closed. The shutters have been slammed on the windows, and W.'s out in the cold, stamping his feet for warmth. And there I am beside him.

What do I want from him?, W. asks. What does he want from himself? Ah, there's no way of telling. He'll simply have to follow where I lead, and listen to what I say. We're heading out, out into the wilderness, he knows that. Out beneath the flashing stars and the silvery pines, to where nothing can survive.

How is it that our idiocy still surprises us?, W. wonders. Is it that we still harbour the hope of overcoming our idiocy?

Who allowed it? Who raised our aspirations to the sky? We want to blame someone. It must be someone else's fault. Our horizons were opened too widely. We saw too much . . . But who let us see? Who left the doorway open?

Suicide by Cop, W. reads a newspaper headline. What of suicide by philosophy?, he says. What of the attempt to incite murder through the extent of one's stupidity? Because that's the only way he can account for us, the shortcomings of our thought. It's the only way he can account for our persistent attempt to think.

There's something entirely lacking in us, W. says, although he's not quite sure what it is. Shame—is that the word? Anyone else would have stopped doing what we do.

There's a short story by Kafka, a fragment really, W. says. A man in a great hurry gets lost on the way to the station and asks a policeman for directions. *Gibt sie auf!*, says the policeman, *Give it up!* That's what we should do, says W. Give it up!

W. never likes to be too far from bodies of water. When he visits me, he always demands to be taken to the sea. And he always takes me directly to the sea, when I visit him. '*I'll meet you at the sea*', he texts me, when I tell him I've arrived. I have to go straight there, straight from the airport to the sea to meet him.

And now, in the middle of America, when the sea's so far away? We feel drawn to the Mississippi. One of the blue-capped tourist guides points the way. Down Beale Street, cross the road . . .

We stand by the roadside, trying to figure out how to get across. Cars pass in an endless stream. Lorries, buses, without a break.

We'll have to run, I tell W. Run! We run, just making the other side. But Sal's been left behind. There she is, waving to us. There's nothing we can do, W. says. She's lost! She'll never make it! We'll have to go on without her.

Still one more road to cross. We follow the same technique: a headlong rushing, closing our eyes as we run. We're madmen! Sal, meanwhile, has found a button you can push to get the traffic lights working. She crosses calmly. Why didn't we work that out? She crosses the second street. —'You twats', she says, 'why did you leave me behind?'

The Mississippi: more than half a mile wide. —'*I think that the river is a strong brown god*', W. says, quoting Eliot. '*Keeping his reasons and rages, destroyer, reminder/ Of what men choose to forget . . .* '

Destroyer indeed. Periodically, the Mississippi breaks the levees and floods the river bottoms where the poor live and work, W. says. That's what happened in the great flood of '27. A million people were displaced. Whole towns were engulfed . . .

They made the poor blacks pay for their aid, of course. And if they couldn't pay? They were confined in work camps, and made to do forced labour . . .

W. presses an earbud into my ear and an earbud into his. We listen to the deep blues of the Delta. Tommy Johnson. Big Joe Williams. We listen to pulsating grooves, barely songs, with no distinct beginning or end, and to verses that speak of turbulence and dislocation, of rootlessness and violent death, of the great flood of '27 and the great drought of '29.

It's the *music of life*, W. says. Of still being alive. Of being torn apart, of being insulted and injured, of being still alive in the one chord vamp, in a rhythm that precedes melody, that breaks and fragments it, dissolving melody in the waters of its own flood.

What would my blues name be?, W. wonders. Hindu Fats, he says. Hindu Fat Boy.

On the banks of the river, Sal takes photos of us for W.'s Facebook page. He rides me like a horse. I ride him like a horse. Sal rides both of us, like two horses, with the camera set on automatic. And behind us, the muddy brown waters of the Mississippi, surging along.

America's so big!, we agree. How far is it to the coast, east or west? A thousand miles? Two thousand? Some great, improbable distance, we're agreed. Some distance of which we cannot conceive.

There's so much space here. America's so exposed. We think of the hurricane damage we saw from the Greyhound bus. Houses torn up, trees uprooted and flung about. I took photos. We'd never seen anything like it. America's in danger, we agree. It's too big! It's too vulnerable!

We think of the coming catastrophe, of the winds that will sweep this country, the deserts that will claim it, the skies that will darken over it. Will it be here that the apocalypse rises to its greatest magnitude?

That's what Josh T. Pearson sings, W. says, tapping his iPod. '*The USA's the centre of JerUSAlem . . .* '

Hope. What is it that keeps us going?, W. wonders. Why do we bother, in spite of it all, in the face of it all?

That we know our limitations is our strength, we're agreed on that. We know we fall short, desperately short. We know our task is too great for us, but at least we have a sense of it, its greatness. At least we know it passes above us, like migratory birds in the autumn sky.

We're *landfill thinkers*, W. says. *Landfill philosophers*. But he doesn't mind. He has the sense of edging forward in the darkness, he says. He has the sense of digging his burrow, of pushing on in dark times.

And what kind of burrow am I digging?, W. wonders. What kind of tunnel can a mole make that is without claws, a mole that's gone mad underground?

In the end, I excel at only three things, W. says: smut, chimp noises and made-up German. That's all my scholarship has amounted to.

And isn't it the same with him? Ah, what does he really

know? Of what is he really certain? Biblical Hebrew, of course . . . The classical guitar . . . The history of philosophy in the German tradition, in the French tradition . . . Something of the ancient Greeks, and the language of the ancient Greeks . . . But it's nothing, nothing, W. says. He knows nothing at all.

If he's cruel to me, it is the same cruelty to which he subjects himself, W. says. If he's cruel, it's out of love, W. says. It is meant as a sign that he expects better. Would that *he* had a similar tutor! Would that he had someone to list *his* betrayals and half-measures!

The pelican of mythology feeds its young by tearing strips of its own flesh from its breast, W. says. And isn't that how he's fed me: by tearing strips of flesh from his own breast?

How generous he's been! How unselfish! But in the end, it's left him even more alone, his generosity. In the end, a great, overfed chick is no company.

The bus back to Nashville. Sounds of screaming. A roaring two-stroke engine. The passenger in front of us is playing *The Texas Chainsaw Massacre* on his laptop.

W. yearns for his study, he says. He yearns for his book-shelves. He yearns for the tranquillity of his mornings, when he leaves a sleeping Sal in bed so that he can do a few hours of work before breakfast.

I understand nothing of the *rhythms* of scholarship, W. says, I know nothing of its *seasons*: of the time of sowing, of tending and caring, and of the harvest, the gathering in of the crops of thought.

Isn't it that of which he dreams, at the beginning of the summer: of the coming autumn, which will see his thought-crops ripe and ready, bowing in the breeze? Of carrying back the harvest of his ideas, so carefully tended, in his sun-browned arms?

There must be a process of thought-threshing, too, W. says. Of thought-winnowing! The wheat must be separated from the chaff. And there will be chaff, he says. Even the greatest of thinkers cannot avoid chaff. But there is still wheat. Still the evidence of a year's long labour . . .

But what would he know of this? His crops have failed, W. says, as they have always failed, and he stands in the empty field, weeping.

Ah, when will we discover the rhythm that will let us work, really work?, W. wonders. When, that steady pressure that will make every day a work day, every day launched with a forward push from the day before . . .

Momentum: to be thrown by thought, loosed, like a stone from thought's sling . . . And work, then, will not be mundane, but celestial. We will work as the stars work, as the planets turn in their orbits. Our work will be as one with the slow turning of galaxies, and the steady expansion of the universe out into the infinite . . . Our work will be indistinguishable from inactivity, from the resting of a God.

Perhaps it is really a kind of Sabbath that we're looking for, W. says. A time to close our eyes; but not only to rest, to recuperate. *We need to contemplate our labours from without and not just from within*: who was it who said that?, he wonders. We need to let ourselves be touched by a greater work, by a divine labour. Isn't it only then that we'll truly begin to work, as though drawn by a hidden current into the centre of our channel?

We must work until we bleed, W. says. We must write until our eyes turn red, and blood runs from our nostrils. Because that's what's going to happen to us when we find our idea: blood will flow from our nostrils. Drops of blood, splashing onto the pages on which we are writing . . .

Of all writings I love only that which is written with blood. Nietzsche wrote that. With blood, but not *our* blood. We'll write with *God*'s blood, says W., mystically. It will be the *blood of God* that runs from our nostrils.

Bored on the bus. W. seizes my notebook. He wants to see how America has advanced my thinking. —'Ah! Drawings! Who's that supposed to be?' Huckleberry Finn, I tell him. There's the raft. —'And what's that in the water next to him?' It's Moby Dick, I tell him. And that's the Pequod. W. admires my *classics of American literature* series.

And what is this? A poem? *Preppies*, it's called.

Tall / sand in the hair / white teeth / pullovers / deck shoes / white shirts and blouses / yachts with white sails / fuckers

Very perceptive, says W. Here's another. *Cabin Boys*, it's called.

Upstairs, on deck / The preppies are dancing / with their caps worn backwards. / We are the cabin boys / scrubbing their things. / We are angry

He likes that, W. says. It's very terse.

And what are these? More poems?', W. asks, turning my notebook upside down and squinting. Lyrics, I tell him. They're lyrics from Jandek.

*I don't care about philosophy / Even if it's right.
I could always go drinking / and never come
back . . .*

Ah, Jandek, W. says. Who else? Sal has thrown away
all the Jandek CDs I burned for him. *The Humility of Pain.*
—'That was his forty-fifth LP, wasn't it?' His forty-sixth, I
tell him.

The Humility of Pain: now there's an album title, W.
says. Jandek has seen things, experienced things, of which we
can have no understanding, he says. He is a man of despair,
of complete despair. But he is a man of God, too. Doesn't
Jandek always gather his musicians for a moment of prayer
before going on stage? 'Lord give us strength . . . Lord protect
us'. We're not capable of God, W. says.

In the end, W. doesn't understand why people believe in God,
or even what they mean by the word. He doesn't have the
insouciance of those who call themselves *atheists*, W. says.
He doesn't know what that word means.

When it comes to God, he keeps feeling he's come up
against something immovable, something through which he
cannot pass. It's not because he thinks there's some mystical knowledge which he cannot quite reach—on the con-
trary—but that there is something he cannot think, something
he cannot see that is called God, and all because of his personal stupidity.

Sometimes, W. dreams of collaborating with me, on a

book on God. He dreams of a great outpouring of his intellect and passion. He dreams of honouring the legacies of Pascal and Weil, and uncovering the meaning of God in Cohen and Rosenzweig. He dreams of making Kierkegaardian leaps, and of foaming at the mouth in Dostoevskian fervour.

And what would I contribute? What would I bring to the project? —'You could explain your indifference', W. says. 'And then you could draw some cocks'.

A rest break in Jackson, in the early hours. Through the bus window, we admire our fellow passengers, standing about in the open air, their breath frosty. Who are they, our fellow travellers? Where are they heading? We are tired, travel-weary, but they're fresh, expectant, ready for the world.

Distance means nothing to the American, W. says. Uprooting! The American rolls across the earth like dice, he says. One minute, the American's married; the next, divorced. Then married again, then divorced again . . . Then starting a new career. Leaving one job, and beginning another on the other side of the state, on the other side of the continent . . .

Americans pack up and go! They move from state to state just like that! They think nothing of travelling vast distances, of relocating themselves, of starting new lives!

W. speaks movingly of the first migrants to America, who crossed via the vanished land bridge from Siberia. Of course, they were hunter-gatherers, he says. The *disaster of agriculture*, to which he traces the origins of capitalism, had not yet happened.

The mid-Neolithic: perhaps that's when it all went wrong, W. muses. Once you have agriculture, you have concentrations of wealth. You have military specialisation! Predation! Man becomes a wolf to man! That's what he's learnt from playing *Civilization 4*, W. says.

Maybe we should become foragers, like our early ancestors. Maybe we should just *go forth*, living on berries and roadkill and whatever else we find. We dream for a moment of wandering across America, like the first wave of migrants who crossed the great landbridge. We dream of living on the fruits of America, on American generosity, the land spreading before us in all its bounty and the pair of us like idiot Whitmans in our blousy shirts.

Pigeon Forge. The end is nigh.

With every mini-golf course or water ride we pass, W. sinks lower. With every giant golden cross on a hilltop, every novelty motel and advert for apocalyptically-themed shows for all the family (*Revelations: the Musical*; *The Seven Seals On Ice* . . .), W.'s cries grow louder. *Kroger's, The Old Time Country Shop*, more huge crosses looming over nowhere . . .

They've made a theme park of the End of Times!, W. says. They've made a *Disneyland* of Armageddon!

W. hears laughter, but he doesn't know from where. He hears laughter filling the air. Are they laughing at him, the Americans? They laughed at Mr Scheitz, and his mad ideas, W. says. They put him in jail. Is that where W.'s going to end up: in jail? And they laughed at Bruno, until he shot himself. Is that what I'm going to do, shoot myself?, W. wonders. —'Don't do it, fat boy!'

Night falls and we're lost in the Smokies, looking for our cabin. Precipices to the left and the right. Our driver-host is edgy. The car's too heavy! We passengers get out and walk — there's ice everywhere, and the road's too steep for the car.

The mountains tower above us. Starlight glitters on the icy road. Are we going to survive? Will we be lost forever in the wilderness? Doesn't Dolly Parton live round here some-where?

Then we see it: the cabin. It's almost too late for W. He's raving. What's he doing here? How did he end up here? He can't go another mile! He's a non-passenger! A non-traveller! Not another mile!

Later, W. collapses on the balcony, still wet from the hot tub: a dying swan, half wrapped in his towels. What's this country doing to him?, he says. How did he end up here? We talk softly to him, over our Plymouth Gins cut with tapwater.

When he recovers, W. speaks movingly of the early blues players. Such short lives! But life is short! There's not much time!

What need was there to come to America?, W. asks. He's learnt nothing here. His thought hasn't advanced. Not one new idea! . . . The United States of *Thought-Robbery*, that's what they should call it, W. says. The United States of *Vastation and Waste* . . .

Newcastle. —'There's no sight finer', W. says of the Tyne Bridge, which skims the roofs of the buildings in the gorge. You could touch its green underside from the highest of the roof-gardens. The streetlamps, painted the same dark green, jut upwards from the bridge sides, one hundred and fifty feet in the air. And the great arch of the bridge rises a hundred feet higher . . .

'You need a project', says W. 'You need something to occupy you'. W. has his scholarly tasks, of course. He's even deigned to collaborate with me. But I've never taken it seriously, our collaboration, not really. I've never risen to the heights he envisaged for me.

Hadn't W. always wanted us to soar together in thought? Hadn't he pictured us in his mind as two larks, looping and darting in flight—two larks, wings outstretched, flights interlaced, interwoven, together and apart; or as two never-resting swifts, following parallel channels in the air . . .

We were never to rest. We'd live on the wing, one exploring this, one that, but always reuniting, always coming together in flight, in the onrush of flight, calling out to one another across the heavens . . .

To think like a javelin launched into space. To think like

two javelins, launched in the same direction, arching through the air. To think as a body would fall, as two bodies would fall — tumbling through space. Thinking would be as inevitable as falling under gravity. Thought would be our law, our fate . . . But we'd fall *upwards* into the sky . . . *upwards* into the heights of thought . . .

And instead? There is no flight: not mine, not W.'s. I am his cage, W. says. I am his aviary. What he could have been, if he'd left me behind! What skies he could have explored! But he knows that this, too, is an illusion, an excuse. He can blame me for everything. *It's my fault*, he can say, even as he knows that nothing would have happened if he were free of me.

'Take me to the sea!', W. cries every time he visits. He has to see the sea! My North Sea is very different from his Atlantic, he says. It even *looks* colder, he says, as it comes into view behind the Priory.

Sometimes we pay to enter the Priory, so W. can see the weathered gravestones, whose inscriptions are no longer legible, and inspect what's left of the bunkers, which are a kind of cousin to those at Jennycliff, with empty sockets where there were once gun placements. But today we're on a mission. W. has to get air into his lungs, he says. And he needs a drink!

We follow the road round to *The Park Hotel*, where we are served by an old waiter in a tuxedo. Chips and mayonnaise in the sun, watched by an old Bassett hound, head on paws. Two pints of beer arrive on a tray, the waiter with a white towel over his forearm. —'To the sea!', W. toasts, as our glasses clink.

We talk of our American adventure, and of what we learned from it. We talk of Marx, and of *Stroszek*. And W. wasn't arrested! And I didn't shoot myself! That we survived at all is a miracle, we agree.

What did we learn from our trip? What was its significance? Sometimes W. thinks that our thoughts are too small. That we're unable to think the *magnitude* of what needs to be thought: its vastness, its ominousness, like the black, heavy clouds that precede a hurricane.

W. dreams of a thought that would move with what it thinks, follow and respond to it, like a surfer his wave. A thought that would inhabit what was to be thought, like a fish the sea — no, a thought that would be only a drop of the sea in the sea, belonging to its object as water does to water.

The thought of God would be made of God, the thought of tears would be wet with tears . . . And the thought of disaster?

W. remembers the story I told him about the Hindu doctrine of the Four Ages.

In the *Age of Gold*, I told him, everyone was content; there were no differences between human beings—no high born or low born; and there was no hatred, no violence. Everyone lived for a hundred years. Heaven and earth were one. No priests were necessary, for the meaning of holy scripture was clear. All souls lived in truth.

In the *Age of Silver*, W. remembers, unhappiness appeared, along with weariness and nostalgia. Rain fell; it was necessary to take shelter in the trees. And lifespans dropped by a quarter. Morality began to atrophy; heaven and earth came asunder. But the scriptures were studied, although the priests no longer understood all they read, and squabbled over their interpretations.

In the *Age of Bronze*, W. remembers, fear appeared, predation. People sheltered in the cities that had sprung up on the plains. Lifespans fell by a further quarter. Lies became common. Virtue guttered like a candle flame in the draft. Heaven and earth broke apart. Priests could make out only a few words of the ancient tongue of the scriptures, and the world no longer asked them for their interpretation of the divine word.

In the *Age of Iron*, our age, there is the dominion of power and war: that's what I told W. Honesty and generosity reside only with the poor, who flee from the cities and hide in the valleys. The rule of virtue gives way to the rule of money. Drought lies upon the land, ashes fill the sky. In our age, I told W., the descendants of priests throw aside the scriptures. What do they understand of the ancient tongue? And what relevance has holy scripture to an age without hope?

But I neglected to tell him about the *Age of Shit*. I didn't tell him about the shape of the age to come, which is becoming clearer and clearer to him. War will be all, devouring all, W. says. Human beings will be like rats, like vermin. And the skies will burn, W. says. He can see them burning.

That's when I will come into my own, the last of the great lineage of Brahmin priests, W. says. That's when I will wear my great grin, as the living abortion of that line, its desecration. That's when I'll perform my cosmic dance, like a strutting, overfed chicken . . .

And then? What comes next? The great flood, W. says. Water and darkness. And then, after many thousands of years, the last avatar of Vishnu — what was his name? Kalkin, I remind him. Kalkin will appear, ready to restore the world, W. says. He'll ride a white horse and wield a fiery sword. And he'll perform the sacrifice that destroys the world and lets a new one rise up in its place. And so the whole cycle will begin again.

The Hindu always thinks in cycles, W. says. —'You're a cyclical people'. This is where he is furthest from the Hindu, he says. He, as a Jew and a Catholic, is essentially *linear*. The meaning of the end times — our end times — is entirely different for him, W. says.

What does the apocalypse mean for the Hindu?, W. wonders. Not judgement, and not redemption. For the Hindu, with his endless cycles, the apocalypse can be only the prelude to a new beginning.

Can the Hindu really — *really* — understand the horror of the apocalypse?, W. wonders. Can he really — *really* — understand the glory of redemption?'

It's what he's long suspected, W. says. We both see horror all around us. We both see chaos and degradation, greed and conflict. But it doesn't touch me, not really. Even our age, the worst of all, will see the birth of another of God's avatars, I have that consolation.

He's alone, W. says. Alone with his despair. But he has the Messiah!, I tell him. Ah, but the Messiah is very different from Kalkin, W. says. —'Besides, messianism is best understood in terms of *time*, not some idiot on a horse'. He'll explain that to me another day, he says.

Whitley Bay, walking between the boarded up sea-front buildings. Something has finished here, we agree. Something is over. But at least they haven't begun the regeneration yet. They're going to turn it into a *cultural quarter*. Imagine that! A *cultural quarter*, where there was once the funfair and the golden sands.

It was the same in the city. W. was unimpressed by the regeneration of the quayside, with its so-called *public art*. Public art is invariably a form of marketing for property development, he says. It's inevitably the forerunner of gentrification.

W. is an enemy of art. We ought to *fine* artists rather than subsidise them, he says. They ought to be subject to systematic purges. He's never doubted we need some kind of Cultural Revolution.

The real art of the city is *industrial*, of course, W. says. Spiller's Wharf. The High Bridge. The four storeys of the flax mill in the Ouseburn Valley . . .

W. likes to imagine the people of the city, the old working class, coming to reclaim the quayside. What need did anchor-smiths and salt-panners have for a *cultural quarter*? Why can't the descendants of the keelmen, of the rope-makers and wagon-drivers, come and retake the new *ghettoes for the rich*? In his imagination, W. says, a great army of Geordies storm along the river, smashing the public art and tearing down the new buildings.

A search and rescue helicopter hovers over the sea. Someone must have gone missing. Someone must have disappeared. As we draw closer, we see an ambulance on the beach, and bodysuited lifeguards running into the water, with floats.

We gather with other spectators along the railings of the promenade. A second helicopter has joined the search, following the edge of the shore where the sand gives way to rock. The currents must be very strong, we surmise. You never know where a body might wash up. A teenage boy, head in hands, sits on the steps of the ambulance with a towel around his shoulders.

The whirling blades of the helicopter leave a shadowy impression on the sea. Beneath it, the lifeguards spread out over a few hundred meters, paddling out on their floats. Sometimes they dive and then reappear. Much higher up, rising at an angle, the second helicopter surveys the whole area. Maybe it has special equipment, a kind of sonar, we speculate.

Two men run onto the beach and take off their clothes. They're drunk. They splash out into the sea, nude, laughing and shouting, the helicopters hovering above them. But when they turn and see the long line of spectators, they become suddenly embarrassed. Shamed, they wade back to the beach, hands cupped over their genitals.

W., doleful as we head back to the station. How much time do we have left?, he wonders. A decade? A century? The trouble is, you can't tell, he says. The conditions for the disaster are here, they're omnipresent, but when will it actually come?

He reads book after book on the destruction of the world. Book after book on the apocalypse. He reads about the futures market. He reads about storm-surges and dry-belts. Then he reads *my* books, W. says, shaking his head. —'Your books! My God!' The conditions for the end are here, W. says, but not the end itself, not yet . . .

W. is greatly susceptible to changes in weather, he says on the phone. He can feel them coming days in advance, he says of the Westerlies that bombard his city. He knows there's a low front out over the Atlantic, ready to hit the foot of England with rain and grey clouds and humidity, and another low front behind that. How's he going to get any work done—any *serious* work?

It's alright for me, he says. I'm in the east of the country, for a start, which means that the weather doesn't linger in the same way. Oh it's much colder, he knows that—he always brings a warm jacket when he stays with me—but it's fresher too; it's good for the mind, good for thought.

But W. can't think, he says. He knows the Westerlies are coming. He knows low pressure's going to dominate the weather for weeks, if not months. Sometimes whole seasons are dominated by Westerlies, which costs him an immense amount in lost time and missed work.

He's still up early every morning, of course. He's still at his desk at dawn. Four AM; five AM—he's ready for work; he opens his books; he takes notes as the sky brightens over Stonehouse roofs. He's there at the inception, at the beginning of everything, even before the pigeons start cooing like maniacs on his window-ledge.

He's up before anyone else, he knows that, but there's still no chance of thinking. Not a thought has come to him in recent months; not one. He's stalled, W. says. There's been an interregnum. But when wasn't he stalled? When wasn't it impossible for him to think? No matter how early he gets up, he misses his *appointment with thought*; no matter how he tries to surprise it by being there before everyone else.

W.'s reading a book of Latin philosophical phrases. —'Ah, here's something that applies to you: *Barba non facit philosophum*. A beard does not make a philosopher'. Then he tests me: What does *eo ipso* mean? What's the difference between *modus tollens* and *modus ponens*? —'*Tabula rasa*: I know you know that. And *conatus* — even you must know that'.

'You don't actually *know* anything, do you?', W. says. 'You've got no *body of knowledge*'. W. has ancient Hebrew, of course, and he can play classical guitar. And there are whole *oeuvres* with which he is familiar. He's read his way through Husserl, for example. He's not entirely bewildered by Leibniz.

Socrates knew he knew nothing: that was his wisdom, and the beginning of all wisdom, W. says. But there's a difference between knowing nothing and *knowing nothing*, he says. There's a difference between knowing you know nothing only to sally forth from your ignorance, and wallowing in your ignorance like a hippo in a swamp.

'You don't want to know', W. says. And I'm drinking to

forget what little I *did* know. There's nothing left for me, he says. Nothing but the empty sky, and the Zen-like emptiness of my head.

I'm always overawed by Oxford, W. knows that. Overawed, and therefore contemptuous. I hate it, W. says, because I love it. It disappoints me, W. says, because I have disappointed it: wasn't I bussed in from my secondary modern to see what a real university was like? Didn't I apply to study here as a student?

'What do you think they made of you?', W. asks. 'What did they make of chimp boy, with his delusions of grandeur?' Did I think I would survive a minute in *Balliol College*? Did I think I'd be punting with the toffs?

W.'s dad, who was very wise, banned him from applying altogether. —You don't belong there!', he told him, and he was right. W. has always been free of any *Oxford influence*, he says. He's free of the *attraction to Oxford*, but also of the *repulsion from Oxford*: he doesn't hate it as I do.

Oxford brings out the Diogenes in me, W. says. I all but assault passers-by. Truth-telling, that's what I call it. Drunken abuse, that's what *he'd* call it, W. says.

The kernel is in Poland, we agree as we walk up the Cowley Road. The secret is in Poland. We run through our memories.

Our Polish adventure! When were we happier? Didn't it all come together there? Wasn't it there that it all began?

There we were, ambassadors for our country, in our teeshirts and jungle-print shorts. There we were, intellectual delegates, given a civic reception. Wasn't it the mayor of Wrocław himself who greeted us? Of course, the welcoming committee in Wrocław looked at us in bemusement: was this the best Britain had to offer?

'And that was before they heard you go on about blow-holes, over dinner', W. says. That was before the real fiasco began, he says, when we re-enacted Freud's *primal scene*, on the dancefloor. It's a British dance move, we told them. It's what we do on British dancefloors. They looked away from us, appalled.

But, in general, the Poles treated us with European grace. We attended a grill party in the sun — that's what they called it, a *grill party*. There were sausages and beer. We British are a loutish people, we told them. Don't expect anything from us. We said we'd disappoint them, we warned them in advance, but, after a while, they seemed to find us charming.

W. thinks we won them over, he says. They came to like our inanities. To them, we were a race apart, like Neanderthals or something. A lower branch on the human tree. Once they knew they could hope for very little, it was okay. We were free from any expectations.

Yes, that's where it all began, W. and I agree. Free from our hosts' expectations, we also became freer from our own. It was then, in our jungle-print shorts, that we accepted what we were.

The Trout, overlooking the meadows.

Oxford: the very name is a blow to W. It strikes him on the head like a bludgeon. It sounds through him like a depth-charge. Oxford!, Oxford!

Why do we come here year after year?, W. says. Why, to our conference, and to wandering from pub to pub after our conference? Why, lamenting the intellectual state of our country, and *our* intellectual state?

Britain is not a country of thought, we tell ourselves every year. The Anglo-Saxon mentality is opposed to abstraction, to metaphysics, we tell ourselves. It is completely opposed to German profundity and French radicality, to Central European *Weltschmerz*, and to Russian *soulfulness* . . . It has nothing to do with Spanish *duende*, or the Greek sense of *fate*.

And above all, the British don't understand *religion*, W. says. They don't understand *religious pathos*. The British are too empiricist, W. says. Too literalist. They don't see that religion's all around them. Religion is about *this* world, about everyday things. That's what the continentalist understands, he says. That's what the new atheist *fails* to understand.

Hasn't W. tried to set up an *alternative intellectual*

network for people like ourselves? Hasn't he run his famous Plymouth conferences, inviting but a handful of speakers to his college, and allowing them to select their ideal interlocutors? Hasn't he wheedled money from all kinds of sources to pay for it all?

Ah, it was marvellous, until I ruined it, W. says. Why did he think of inviting me?, he says, shaking his head as we sip our pints. He still remembers it, the whole afternoon devoted to my work, to my so-called work. The thing is, the audience — my invited audience — were on my side to begin with, W. says. —'They wanted you to do well'. But what happened? He shakes his head.

Why did he invite me?, W. wonders. There'd be sense in bringing people to his college to inspire him, but not to destroy him. Unless it's his death-drive, W. says. Unless *I'm* his death-drive, for how else could he account for it?

I ruined his conference, there's no question of that, W. says. I ruined his whole series of conferences. And what choice did he have but to return to Oxford, to our Oxford conference, and with me in tow? What, but to rejoin the would-be Oxonians, who hire out the college of St. Hilda's when all the real Oxford academics are away?

Philosophy's like an unrequited love affair, W. says. You get nothing back; there's only longing, inadequacy, a life unfulfilled. But sometimes he feels he might be capable of philosophy. That *we* might be capable of it, together — together with our friends.

Didn't he have friends once?, W. says. I drove them away, of course. They ran away in horror. What is W. doing?, they wondered. They wrote him emails. Didn't he realise he was *ruining his reputation*?

Ah, why does he hang out with me?, W. says. It's not as if he has no options. He *chooses* to hang out with me, that's the thing. It's his choice — or is it? Is it an instinct? Is it the *opposite* of an instinct?

Either way, he remains in my labyrinth, W. says. His fear: he'll stay there, getting more and more lost, lost until he's forgotten he's *in* a labyrinth. I'm becoming his world, says W. His whole world, and isn't that the horror?

He's like an actor who's forgotten he's acting. A secret agent in the deepest of cover. He doesn't know who he is anymore. A denizen of Larsworld, that's it, isn't it? Another of my nutters and weirdoes . . .

We need a *realitätpunkt*, W. says. A point of absolute certainty, from which everything could begin. But the only thing of which he can be certain is the eternal crumbling of our foundations, the eternal stop sign of our idiocy.

Every day is only the fresh ruination of any project we might give ourselves. Every day, the fresh revelation of our limitations and of the absurdity of our ambitions. What have we learnt except that we have no contribution to make, nothing to say, nothing to write, and that we have long since been outflanked by the world, overtaken by it, beaten half to death by it?

What's happened to them now, his friends?, W. says. They're scattered to the four winds, he says. They're fighting their own battles against redundancy, as he is fighting his. And they're applying, like him, for the tiny number of jobs which appear in the newspapers.

Crowd rats into smaller and smaller spaces, and they turn on one another, devouring one another, W. says, as we pass beneath the Bridge of Sighs. That's what'll happen to us, and to our friends, he says. We'll turn on one another, devouring one another . . .

It's the opposite of everything W.'s hoped for. He dreamed we could stand shoulder to shoulder with them all, with all our friends; and that, standing together, we would form a kind of phalanx, stronger than we would be on our own. He dreamed we'd mated for life like swans, and that we could no more betray one another than tear off our own limbs . . .

We speak of thinker-collectives over our pints in *The Turf*. Of Hegel, Hölderlin and Schelling dancing round their freedom tree. Of Novalis and the Schlegels, practicing their *symphilosophical* collaboration on the streets of Jena. We speak of Marx, Engels and other revolutionary émigrés, on the run from the police of continental Europe, holed up in London after the failed revolutions of 1848.

And we speak, coming to the twentieth century, of artistic avant-gardes, of Surrealism and the Situationists, with their manifestos and expulsions. Who was more fierce than André Breton? Who, more demanding than Guy Debord? Antonin Artaud ate too loudly — expel him from the group! Asger Jörn kept picking his nose — excommunicate him at once!

Rules: that's what we need, W. says. We need to be constrained. We need a *prime mover*. We need a mastermind to crack the whip. —'Lapdogs', he'll shout. 'Lackeys!'

And if we can find no leader to impose discipline on us, we must impose it on ourselves, W. says. We must become each other's intellectual conscience. We must become each other's leader, and each other's follower.

W. speaks of the *liberating constraint* sought by the members of OULIPO — Perec, Roubaud and the rest — with their famous rules, which they use to compose literary works. Palindromes, lipograms, acrostics and all that . . . OULIPO's work is *collaborative*, that's the point, W. says. Its products are attributed to the group.

Didn't Queneau call Oulipians *'rats who will build the labyrinth from which they will try to escape?'*, W. says. We are those rats, we agree. We need liberation. But first, we need to build a labyrinth.

We speak of the so-called 'vow of chastity' of Dogme95 — of Lars Von Trier and his friends — who banned all artifice in the making of their films. No stage sets, no blue screen, no CGI dinosaurs or period pieces of any kind. No score; no weeping violins.

Films have to descend to the everyday, and tell stories about the everyday, that's what Dogme95 demanded, W. says. Films have to concern themselves with reality. With love. With death. —'Pathos!', W. says. 'It's all about pathos!'

Dogma: that's what we should call our intellectual movement, we agree. We should make our own 'vow of chastity', our own manifesto. On Magdalen Bridge, leaning over the Cherwell, we cry out our rules over the water.

First rule: Dogma is *spartan*. Speak as clearly as you can. As *simply* as you can. Do not rely on proper names when presenting your thought. Do not quote. Address others. *Really* speak to them, using ordinary language. Ordinary words!

Second rule: Dogma is full of *pathos*. Rely on emotion as much as on argument. Tear your shirt and pull out your hair! And weep — weep without end!

Third rule: Dogma is *sincere*. Speak with the greatest of seriousness, and only on topics that *demand* the greatest of seriousness. Aim at maximum sincerity. Burning sincerity. *Rending* sincerity. Be prepared to set yourself on fire before your audience, like those monks in Vietnam.

And the *fourth* rule? Dogma is *collaborative*. Write with your friends. Your very friendship should depend on what you write. It should mean nothing more than what you write!

W. reminds me of the collection, *Radical Thought in Italy*. Paolo Virno! Mario Tronti! They've always been a touchstone for him. It's pure Dogma, he says. They're all friends. Their essays have no quotations, no references, they all have the same ideas and write about them as though they were *world-historical*. That's another rule, W. says: always write as though your ideas were world-historical. And always steal from your friends. Steal from everyone! In fact, that should be compulsory: Dogma *plagiarises*. Always steal other people's ideas and claim them as your own.

A free man should walk slowly, that's what the Greeks thought, says W. The slave hurries, but the free man can take all day. —'Slow down!', he tells me, as we wander out through the meadows to *The Trout*. I know nothing of *the art of the stroll*, W. has always said. I know nothing of the pleasures of the flâneur.

W.'s always had a messianic faith in the walker. No one is more annoyed than he by the channelling that forces the pedestrian through a predetermined route. For this reason, W. has always hated airports. There's only ever one direction in an airport, he says. And if you're allowed to wander away, it is only to tempt you to buy things from the innumerable shops.

Doesn't Newcastle airport channel every traveller through a shop floor? It scandalises him, W. says. He wants to knock every bottle of perfume from the rack. He wants to smash every overpriced bottle of wine. But here, today, in the meadows? Every direction is open to us, he notes. We can walk wherever we like and as slowly as we please.

We remember Mandelstam's great walks through the streets of St Petersburg, before he was imprisoned for his poem about Stalin, and murdered in the Gulag. He composed poems in his head as he walked. He wrote them in his head, as he walked along, and then went home to write them out. And when he was betrayed, and his manuscripts destroyed, his wife stowed them in *her* head. A precious cargo.

W. knew I was a would-be *man of culture* when he saw her memoir *Hope Against Hope* on my bookshelf. It didn't matter to W. whether I'd read it or not, or whether I had any real idea of what it contained. The title itself must have excited me: that was enough for W. The title, and the *myth* of Mandelstam, exiled from his city and murdered in the Gulag: I had a feeling for that; what else could W. ask for in a collaborator, in these fallen times?

Celan, in the midst of his walks, would phone his wife with the poems he had written in his head, W. remembers. And didn't Celan claim to have seen God under the door of his hotel room? He saw God as a ray of light under his hotel door, W. says, it's very moving.

Ah, but what sense can we have of Mandelstam, of Celan? What can we understand of poetry, in the *Age of Shit*? In the end, we love only the *myth* of poetry, the myth of the *world-historical importance* of poetry, and the myth of ourselves as readers of poetry . . .

We love poetry because we have no idea about poetry, W. says. We love religion because we have no idea about religion. We love God because we have no idea of God . . .

There's Walser, too, the patron saint of walkers, W. says. Walser, walking in the Swiss Alps. Walser, who'd long since devoted his time to being mad, rather than writing: he knew his priorities. He was mad, and the mad walked. And one day — fifty years ago, nearly to the day — they found him dead in the snow. He'd walked his way to death. Which is to say, says W., he'd met death on his own terms, far from his mental asylum. And that's exactly his point, W. says. The walker meets the world on his own terms. The walker — the *slow* walker — meets the world according to his measure, W. says.

Ah, if only we were as wise as Walser, that is to say, as *mad* as Walser. If only we understood that our duty is to walk, not to write, merely to walk and not to think. To give up thinking! To give up writing! To give up our *reading*, which is really only the *shadow* of reading, the search for the world-historical importance that reading once had. But we go on, don't we? We collect our books. We surround ourselves with them, the names of Old Europe, when we should have been walking, just that, all along.

It's time for his nap, W. says as we head back to town. Time to go back to his room for his *power nap*, as he calls it. He learned about *power naps* from a public lecture at the university. Sleep for twenty minutes, and you fool the mind into thinking you've been asleep for much longer. Twenty minutes! That's all he needs to regain his composure, W. says.

But I never let him nap, W. says. In fact, I scorn his desire to nap and even the very notion of a nap. I keep him up all night with my inanities, W. says, and then I keep him awake all day with *more* inanities.

Of course, he's the one who insists that we stay up later than anyone else, that we follow the night through all the way until dawn, W. says. How many nights have ended for us just as dawn was brightening the sky, and the first birds were starting to sing? How many nights, with *Stroszek* on the TV and *The Star of Redemption* open on the desk?

W. is a man who wants to *see the night through* he says. But the afternoon . . . that's my time, W. concedes. That's when I come into my own. When everyone around me is tired and can put up no defence. When everyone's too tired to make me shut up, that's Lars-time, W. says. —'That's when you pounce'. The afternoon: it's when I'm at my strongest and he's at his weakest, W. says. It's when I can really get going. It's when I wear everyone out.

But it's also when I'm most afraid, of course, that's what I've told him, W. says. He's always been struck by that: for him, the afternoon is a time of repose, for the gathering of strength, but for me, it's a time of fear.

It must be my years of unemployment, W. says. Didn't I tell him my afternoons used to sag like a *drooping washing line*? Didn't I complain of the *eternullity* of those afternoons, of their *infinite wearing away*? It was post-*Neighbours* time, the afternoon, that's what I told him. Post *This Morning*, post *Kilroy*, and deep into the time of American cop-show repeats.

Columbo-time, W. says, I could never bear that, could I? Instead I'd go out for walk, that's what I told him. Instead, it was time for a bike ride. Anything to be active! Anything to have something to do! I'd head up to *Tesco* for discounted sandwiches, wasn't that it? I'd head into the library for another video, all the time full of fear, all the time anxious about—what? How did I put it? *The infinite wearing away*, I said, quoting Blanchot. *Eternullity*, I said, quoting Lefebvre.

It's no wonder I'm no night-owl, W. says. No wonder that I'm always worn out by dinnertime. I always revive myself, when I visit him, with a slab of Stella and some pork scratchings. That's my pre-dinner snack.

W., meanwhile, would have been refreshed from his nap, if I'd allowed him to sleep. He would have come downstairs, a man refreshed, reborn, having had a power-nap, he says.

But instead, I insist on conversation, W. says. I insist on wearing him out: he lying on the sofa; I, sitting up at the table. I insist we make some wild plan or other, W. says.

For me, the afternoon's always planning-time, *world-conquest-time*, as W. calls it. I have to pretend to some kind of hold on the future, W. has noticed. It's like a climber throwing up a grappling hook, or Spiderman swinging by his squirted webs. I'm never *happy in the moment*, W. says. I'm never happy *in the belly of the afternoon*.

St Hilda's College, looking at the river. Capitalism and religion, W. muses. He hasn't got much further with his thinking, he says. His notebook's nearly empty. I flick through it.

Where there is hope there is religion: Bloch, I read. *Sometimes God, sometimes nothing: Kafka*, I read. *I have seen God, I have heard God: a ray of light under the door of my hotel room: Celan*. Beautiful! But there are few thoughts of W.'s own. He's going through a dry period, W. says.

Maybe he should try his hand at poetry, like me, W. says. He could write haiku: '*Half ton friend / in trouble again*'. '*Fuckwit in a vest / Friend I love best*'. Or he could draw some pictures. *Study for a Divvy. Landscape with Idiot.*

Here's his favourite quotation, W. says. They should put it on his gravestone. It's by Hermann Müller, he says. It's called 'The Luckless Angel':

The past surges behind him, pouring rubble on his wings and shoulders and thundering like buried drums, while in front of him the future collects, exploding his eyeballs, strangling him with his breath. The luckless angel is silent, waiting for history in

*the petrification of flight, glance, breath. Until the
renewed rush of powerful wings swelling in waves
through the stones signals his flight.*

Sometimes, W. thinks it's fallen to us: the great task of preserving the legacy of Old Europe. It's our task, he thinks, our allotted mission, to keep something alive of continental Europe in our benighted country, W. says.

Ah, how was it coupled in us, the fear and loathing of the present world *and* the messianic sense of what it might have been?, W. wonders. How, in us, are combined the sense that our careers — our lives as so-called thinkers — could only have been the result of some great collapse, *and* the conviction that we are the preservers of a glorious European past, and that we have a share in that past?

How, in us, was joined the sense that our learning — which is really only an *enthusiasm* for learning, for our philosophy, for literature—is of complete irrelevance and indifference, *and* the mad belief that our learning bears upon what is most important and risky of all, upon the great questions of the age?

We're delusional, W. says. He knows that. We've gone wrong, terribly wrong, he knows that, too. But don't we belong to something important, something greater than us, even if we are only its grotesque parody?

We're hinderers of thought, W. says. We trip it up, humiliate it. There's thought, flat on the floor. There it is, drunk as we are drunk and throwing up over the side of the bridge . . .

But thought is here, right here, very close to us, that's the thing, W. says. Thought's here, it must be desperate. There must be no one else for thought to hang out with. We're its last friends, W. says. We're *the last friends of thought* . . .

In his imagination, W. says, our offices in our cities at the edges of this country are like the Dark Age monasteries on the edge of Europe, keeping the old knowledge alive. In his imagination, our teaching is samizdat, outlawed because it is dangerous, the secret police infiltrating our lectures and preparing to take us away. In W.'s imagination, the enemies of thought are tracking us even here, even in Oxford. *Especially* in Oxford. They're watching. They invited us here to keep us close. To press us close to the bosom of Oxford. To suffocate us. To suck the life out of us . . .

But in reality, W. knows no one is watching. No one cares anymore, that's the truth of it, W. says. No one's on the look out. There was no guard on the door of St Hilda's College. There's no one who could regard us as interlopers.

It's like Rome after it was sacked by the Barbarians, says W. They've come and gone, the Barbarians, the wreckers of civilisation. And now there's no guard; there's nothing to protect. We're inside — yes; but that is only a sign that there is no longer a distinction between inside and outside.

We've got away with nothing; our stupidity is in plain view. It doesn't matter; it's irrelevant to everyone. No one's worried about our credentials, because there are no credentials. There's only luck. And opportunism. Were we lucky?, I ask him. —'Undoubtedly'. And were we opportunists? —'We were too stupid to be opportunists'.

He sees it, W. says, like an enormous fact. A great fact, like the wide sky, that says: *it doesn't matter*. Over the Bodelian Library, it says: *it's all over*. Over the college quadrangles, it says: *it's finished. You're too late*. Over the gowned academics, it says: *Gibt sie auf! Gibt sie auf! Gibt sie auf!*

The gate stands open. It's nearly falling from its hinges. And beyond it, other doors, or gaps in walls where there were once doors, or rubble where there were once walls, or mounds of dust where there was once rubble. And beyond that: empty space without stars. Nothing at all.

Rolling thunder. Lightning flashing in the summer sky. There's trouble at his college, W. says.

The rumour is they're going to close down all the humanities, every course. The college is going to specialise in sport instead. They've brought in a team of consultants to manage the redundancies, W. says.

Oh, some staff will be kept on, they've said that. The college needs some academic respectability. They'll probably make him a *professor of badminton ethics*, W. says. He'll probably be teaching *shot put metaphysics* . . .

But everyone will have to reapply for their jobs, that's the rumour. They're going to cut the workforce in half. It's Hobbesian, W. says. There's going to be a war of all against all.

How peaceful it was, his college, when he first arrived! Colleagues greeted each other warmly. They sat out in the quadrangle, taking tea and discussing their scholarship. No one taught for more than a couple of hours a week.

Then the decline began. Teaching hours went up.

Colleagues became busier; there was less time to talk. Scholars worked alone, with their office doors closed. But still they waved at one another across the quadrangle. Still, when they had time, they visited each other's offices for tea.

But things fell further. Colleagues did nothing but teach, W. says. No one spoke. No one took tea. Scholars — what scholars were left — worked alone, talking to no one, keeping their insights to themselves. The quadrangle was silent.

And now? Colleagues have forgotten what scholarship is. They've forgotten anything but teaching, endless, remorseless teaching. Former scholars snarl at each other in the college corridors. And there are rumours that the library will be torched, and that they'll set up a gallows in the quadrangle. It's like something out of Dante, W. says.

The war is beginning, W. says. The armies are assembling. It's as though the awful Hindu stories I tell are coming true. He feels like Arjuna in the great battle of the *Mahabharata*, W. says. He feels like the leader of the Pandavan armies on the Kurukshetra plains, facing his friends and relatives on the opposing side.

Uncle was set against nephew, that's what I told him, isn't it?, W. says, pupil against teacher, friend against friend: the battle had torn families apart, old friendships asunder . . . Arjuna threw aside his bow and sank to his knees, I told W. Why should he fight?, he cried to his friend, Krishna. Why should he go on? And that's what W. wails when he's with me: why should *he* fight? Why should *he* go on?

W. is going to commence hostilities with scholar-brothers from the old days, when his college was a place of reputation, when the department of theology and philosophy was the jewel in its crown. He's heading into battle with scholar-sisters from the times when the college was a place of sanctuary for academics from overseas: when they took in scholar-refugees, scholar-survivors from war-torn countries, giving them an office in which to work, and a pass for the library.

W.'s about to skirmish with fellow scholars of ancient civilisations, fellow men and women of the archive, who have spent their lives travelling from place of learning to place of learning. He's pitted against scholars mesmerised by Old Europe, as he is. Mesmerised by Kafka, mesmerised by Spinoza. Mesmerised by the French and the German and the ancient Greeks . . .

Krishna comforted Arjuna by granting him a divine vision, W. recalls. Arjuna was allowed to witness Krishna's celestial form: to see the entire cosmos turning in his body. Arjuna saw the light of God, the Lord of Yoga, as a fire that burns to consume all things. He saw a million divine figures in the fire, and the manifold contours of the universe united as one . . .

'What does your celestial form look like?', says W. 'Go on, show me'. Actually, he thinks he's already seen it, W. says, or parts of it. My vast, white belly. My flabby arms. The trousers that billow round my ankles . . .

And my dancing, my terrible dancing. It's the *end* of the

cosmos that W. sees in my dancing. He sees the *destruction* of the divine figures, and of the manifold contours of the universe. He sees *primordial chaos*, he says. He sees the putting out of the stars. He sees the extinguishing of the sun, and the night swallowing the day. He sees the opposite of the act of creation, the opposite of cosmogony . . .

'*The floodgates of the sky broke open*', he says, quoting *Genesis*. He sees '*the waters of the great Deep*', and '*the Dragon of the Sea*', he says, quoting *Isaiah*.

How does the *Mahabharata* end?, W. asks. *And darkness fell over India*, I remind him. —'You Hindus have a great sense of decline. *And darkness fell over India* . . . ', he sighs. 'That's the way to end an epic'.

Our inaugural Dogma presentation was on Kafka — the room was packed, and W. spoke very movingly of his encounter with *The Castle* in a Wolverhampton library. I spoke (very ineptly, W. said afterwards) about my encounter with *The Castle* in a Winnersh Triangle warehouse. —'What were you on about?' But Dogmatists stick together; a question for one is a question for the other. You have to stand back to back and fight to the last. Did we win? We lost, says W., but we did so gloriously.

Our *second* Dogma presentation concerned friendship as a condition of thought. W. stole half his argument from Paolo Virno, and the other half from Mario Tronti. Virno and Tronti write of their ideas as though they were categories in Aristotle, W. says. He admires that. W. reminds me of the sixth Dogma rule: always claim the ideas of others as your own.

Forming an ultra-Dogmatist splinter group, I spoke not of friendship in general, but of *my* friendships (my friendships with nutters and weirdos, W. says.)

W. is prompted to add another rule to Dogma: Dogma is *personal*. Always give examples from your own experience. No: the presentation *in its entirety* should begin and end with an account of your own experience. Of turning points! Trials! Of great struggles and humiliations! My life lends itself particularly well to such a rule, W. says. —'The horror of your life'.

Our *third* Dogma presentation was perhaps our pinnacle. Did we weep? Very nearly. Did we tear open our shirts? It was close. Did we speak with the greatest seriousness we could muster—with *world-historical* seriousness? Of course! And did we take questions for one another like a relay team, passing the baton effortlessly to and fro? Without doubt!

W. spoke of nuns; I, of monks. He spoke about dogs; I, about children. We thought the very stones would weep. We thought the sky itself would rain down in tears. W. invents a new Dogma rule: always speak of nuns, and dogs.

In our *fourth* Dogma presentation, we spoke of love, the greatest topic of all, says W. But there can be no love in the modern world, W. says, there can be no such thing as love. I spoke of my years with the monks, of divine love and mundane love. I spoke of *agape* and *eros*. And then W. spoke of *philein*: the greatest kind of love, he said.

We were like a tag team, we agreed afterwards. Like two wrestlers succeeding each other in the ring. We should always use Greek terms in our presentations, W. says. That should be another Dogma rule: always use Greek terms that you barely understand.

Sometimes, in my company, W. feels like Jane Goodall, the one who did all that work with chimps. Jane Goodall, the chimp specialist, who not only studied chimps, but went to live with chimps, among them, slowly gaining their confidence and learning their ways.

What has he learnt about me through his studies?, W. wonders. What's become clear to him? Admittedly, he first approached me as a collaborator. Here is a man with whom I can think, he told himself. Here is a *companion in thought*.

Wasn't I the one he'd been waiting for? Wasn't I a thinker like he was, of the same cast, with the same inclinations, the same distastes? I had a lower IQ than his, of course, but I was quick. I spoke well. My voice resounded beneath vaulted ceilings. Some seemed to have hopes for me. I was going somewhere, they thought. And W. concluded the same.

W. sought a *thought-partner*, but what happened? He became a witness to my decay, he says. He saw me spinning into space like a lost satellite. I squandered it all, didn't I? Or perhaps it was never there — W. wonders about that too. Perhaps it was never there, my talent, my ability. Perhaps it was entirely a *mirage*, being only what W. wanted to see.

A *thought-companion*, that's what W. wanted. And

instead what has he become? A kind of zoo-keeper, he says. A chimp specialist.

For our *fifth* Dogma presentation, W. wrote two quotations on the blackboard, and we sat in silence. '*Man must be torn open again and again by the plowshare of suffering*', he wrote. '*Death is not overcome by not dying, but by our loving beyond death*', he wrote.

For our *sixth*, W. contented himself with a single quotation: the words Sorel was supposed to have said on his deathbed. '*We have destroyed the validity of all words. Nothing remains but violence*'. For the *seventh*, but a single word was necessary, projected onto the wall behind us: *DERELICTION*.

Spital Tongues, Newcastle. —'God, your flat is filthy', W. says. 'You don't have any idea how to clean, do you?' W. suspects it's a Brahminical thing. I can't do any menial labour! I'm too pure to clean. I can't *get down on my hands and knees*.

Detachment, that's what I'm cultivating, W. says. The maximum possible tension between outside (the squalor of the flat) and inside (the ultimate self, *Atman*). And this tension is like a drawn bow, ready to shoot me towards enlightenment, W. says.

'What's that noise', W. asks. 'Is it squeaking?' Rats, I tell him. Rats have infested my flat. I point out the rat droppings in the yard—black, elongated pellets, ten or twelve of them, some forming a haphazard pile, others scattered. I point out the soil displaced from the plant pots. The rats have been looking for bulbs to eat.

Another squeak, like strangled birdsong. —'Where's it coming from?', asks W. 'Inside the flat?' Beneath it, I tell him. That's where they live now, the rats.

There's a five foot gap beneath the floorboards, I tell him, all the way down to the mud. The other day, I pulled up one of the floorboards and shined a light down there. I saw the rats, I tell W. I don't know how many there are. I don't know what they were doing. But I could see them crawling over each other, I tell him. I could see their wet fur glistening.

'What are they doing down there?', asks W., shuddering. 'What do they eat?' And then, 'You're feeding them, aren't you? You're *cultivating* them'. He reminds me of the narrator of Trakl's poem, who feeds rats in a twilit yard, in an act that betrays all of humankind.

He can see it in my face, he says, in the madness of my eyes: the dream of *murine becomings*, of *feral alterity*: of rat packs, alive with fleas, spreading out from my flat, crawling, burrowing, swimming in all directions, bearers of new kinds of plague . . .

Rats come from the East, W. says. They come from the deserts of Arabia (the black rat) and the shores of Lake Baikal (the brown rat), thriving in periods of war and famine, and spreading epidemics of plague as they move westwards.

They reached Britain in the thirteenth century (the black rat) and in the nineteenth century (the brown rat), being omnivorous, adaptable, fecund. Rats are pitiless, W. says (the brown rat more than the black rat). Merciless. They drive the weak before them. Just as the black rat drove out its natural rivals, so the brown rat drove out the black rat. And no doubt, there are new rat-waves to come . . .

And they're intelligent, too. The brown rat is claimed to

show signs of *meta*-intelligence, though W.'s not sure what that means. He thinks it's got something to do with learning from your mistakes, which is something we've never done. Brown rats are more intelligent than us, W. says, that's the trouble. —'Well, more intelligent than *you*'.

W. tells me of the rat man of Freud's case study, who spoke of his greatest fear, which was also his greatest desire: to have a pot placed on his arse, into which a pack of rats was introduced. His fear, his desire, was for the rats to bore their way in, for them to swarm through his body . . .

   Is that what I want?, W. wonders. Am I, too, waiting for the *rat punishment*? Or perhaps that's why I've invited him up, to rat-punish *him* . . .

I look ill, W. says. Grey. —'What do you think is wrong with you?' Is it the plaster dust, continually falling from the ceiling? Is it the filth on the kitchen counter, or the cans of stale beer? Is it the fact that the whole flat is tilting sideways, like the deck of a ship in a storm?

It's the yard, W.'s sure of it. The shore of concrete, at the same level as the window, covered in algae. —'It's like the end of the world out there', W. says. Dead plants, no more than sticks in pots. The long crack in the kitchen wall, which lets in the rain. The mould-encrusted hopper, overrunning with water.

Then there's the damp, the omnipresent damp. It's no wonder that I cough constantly. Even he, W., has a cough, and he's only visiting for the weekend. He's staggering around like Widow Twankey. How can I do it to him? How can I do it to myself?

Why is he drawn back to my flat again and again? Why does he want to see *where it happens*, or fails to happen?

Ruination, W. says. Living destruction. The Jews have a name for it, W. says: the *tohu vavohu*. The chaos that preceded the act of creation. He supposes the Hindus have a name for it, too, W. says. Actually, he supposes Hinduism *is* a name for it.

'You drink too much, that's your problem', W. says. 'Mind you, I'd drink if I had your life'.

My instincts are wrong, W. says. They always have been. How else can I account for the horror of my life, with its lurches and shudders? How else can I account for that *desire for ruination* that has marked every one of my relationships?

It's going to end in a stabbing, W.'s always said. Someone's going to stab me. But if not him, then who? —'One of your nutters and weirdoes', he says. I know enough of them. —'You've been stabbed before, haven't you?' Nearly, I tell him. —'Well, next time, they'll really get you'.

'My God, your friends', W. says, though he would hardly call them friends. Outpatients. Case studies. —'What do you think they see in you? What do you see in them?' I draw them to me, my nutters and weirdoes. I can never get rid of them. —'You're too weak. Too passive'. I regard myself as *an object to which things happen*, W. says. I call it fate. He calls it idiocy.

Is he one of them, one of my nutters and weirdoes? It's his greatest fear, W. says.

You ought to know everything about your home city, W. says, if only to know what you're about to lose. It makes it more poignant, more mournful, W. says: your loss of your city. Because we will both lose our cities, W. says, it's inevitable. Just as he will be forced out of Plymouth, I will be forced out of Newcastle. Just as he will be kicked out of the city he loves, I will be expelled from the city I *profess* to love, despite the fact that I know nothing about it.

W. had to piece together the history of Newcastle for himself, he says. Perpetually hungover, perpetually dazed, I can scarcely navigate my way to my office. But W. read tour guides and websites; he consulted plaques on our walks. He traced the course of the culvetted rivers that run beneath the streets and speculated upon where they flow out into the Tyne. He consulted Ordinance Survey maps of the riverbanks and insisted upon reconstructing the medieval city in his own mind, walking the route where he thought the city walls must once have run.

Crossing Warwick Street, W. demands we stop at a plaque detailing the construction of the culvert that runs beneath our feet. Heaton once meant 'high-town', we discover, being separated from the city by a steep valley. They filled in the valley and culvetted the river. Why are they always culvetting rivers in Newcastle?, W. wonders.

W.'s decline is getting worse, he says, as we cross the stadium. He doesn't work at night any more, but watches trash TV instead. And now, like me, he's downloaded *Civilization 4*. What appals him, he says, is that he plays *Civilization 4* with more seriousness than he works.

Of course, W. knew that the last thing he should ever do is buy *Civilization 4*. Which meant that he went straight out and bought *Civilization 4*, W. says. Then he destroyed *Civilization 4*; he snapped the CD in two. Then the next morning, he went out and bought it again, he says, but he threw the whole package in the bin before he even got home.

Then, in a weak moment, despairing of his many years of intellectual work and convinced he'd taken a *fundamentally wrong turn in his philosophy*, he downloaded *Civilization 4* from a torrent site, W. says, and has been playing it ever since.

Having Leonard Nimoy as a narrator is an attraction, of course, W. says. Whenever you discover a new technology in *Civilization 4* , it's Leonard Nimoy who speaks some apposite quotation. It's edifying, W. says. He hears Leonard Nimoy's voice now whenever he reads philosophy, he says. '*It is necessary to know whether we are being duped by morality*,' W. reads, in Leonard Nimoy's voice. '*It is the nature of reason to perceive things under a certain species of eternity*,' W. reads, in Leonard Nimoy's voice.

The great philosophers we've heard have always had unfeasibly *high* voices, we agree. Think of Heidegger, on that CD W. bought in Freiburg, going on about Hölderlin. He sounded like a castrati, W. says, and does an impression. '*Sein und Schiesse. Ich bin ein Scheissekopf'*.

Then there was Levinas. Didn't W. phone him once, from a Paris phonebooth? He was going to ask about attending the Talmudic reading classes. But he had to put the phone down when Levinas answered, W. says. His voice was so high! The receiver fell from his hand, with Levinas saying, '*allo? allo?*' in his very high voice.

We find the spot where the Ouseburn re-emerges from the wooded cliff of the filled-in valley. It's not much of a river, W. says, but it's a river nonetheless.

We admire the factory buildings that line the river, and the gaily-coloured boats marooned on the mud banks. *The Toon-tanic*, W. reads on the side of one of the boats.

'You're not one of those happy fat men, are you?', W. says in *The Cumberland*. He always thought being fat made you happy, he says, but I just look sulky.

W. is cheerful and full of bonhomie. Why shouldn't he be? The apocalypse is imminent, things are coming to an end, but in the meantime...? It's always the meantime in the pub, W. says. There's always time enough, when you're drinking.

We stop for another pint at *The Tyne*, and for another in the garden of *The Free Trade*, looking upriver to the city.

W. admires the view. Of course, they'll put up some

great building to spoil it, it's inevitable, just as new flats are planned for the empty lot behind us. —'Flats for yuppies', W. says. Flats for yuppies and preppies, spawning like rats in pastel sweaters . . .

But W. is reassured when I take him through Byker Wall—the legendary Byker Wall—where the city planners tried to make a *Scandinavia* of Newcastle, building social housing in the Danish style. —'Scandinavian social democracy!', W. says, in admiration. 'It's the one positive contribution your people have made to the world'.

It's a shame that my Danish genes triumph over my Indian ones, W. says. It's a shame that umpteen generations of Danish trailer-trash completely overrun the noble line of Brahmin priests.

W. sees my Danish relatives in his mind's eye. Blonde beasts in vests, W. says, belching in the fjords.

Alcohol ruins us, W. says. Pubs ruin us. Ah, what he might have been if he had never drunk! What he might have been, if he hadn't discovered the bar in Essex University Student Union!

Of course, once you reach a certain age, once you're old enough to look round at the world, there's nothing for you to do but drink, W. says. Once you understand that you live in the *age of shit*, there's nothing else for you.

W. reminds me of the fragmentary conversation in Dostoevsky's notebook:

—'*We drink because there is nothing to do*'. —'*You lie! It's because there's no morality*'. —'*Yes, and there is no morality because for a long time, there has been nothing to do*'.

We've *nothing to do*: isn't that our problem?, W. wonders. There's no morality: doesn't that describe our condition? We don't understand what it is to work. We don't understand what it means to be *good* . . .

There is no *grandeur* to my drinking, that's what he objects to, W. says, as we nurse our pints in *The Cumberland*. I should be falling off my barstool, like the drunks in the opening shot of Tarr's *Werckmeister Harmonies*. In some important sense, I haven't *followed through*, W. says. I'm not consistent. I'm hopeful, despite myself.

I must have some instinct for self-preservation, W. says. I must have something within me that holds me back from the abyss.

What's my secret?, W. wonders. What sustains my existence from moment to moment, given that my certainty that *life is shit* should give me no such sustenance whatsoever?

An idiot drools: that's my life, that drooling, W. says. An idiot scratches his head: that's my life, that scratching.

Do I understand, really understand, *the reality of my situation?*, W. wonders. Of course not; it would be quite impossible. I'm not really aware of myself, says W., which is my saving grace. Because if I were . . .

It's enough that W. knows. It's enough that he's aware of *the reality of my situation*. When he tells others about it, they scarcely believe him; they have to blot it out. When he tells them about *the reality of my situation*, they think only of blue skies and summer days, of childhood holidays and birthday parties . . .

Glee: that's what W. always sees on my face. That I'm still alive, that I can still continue, from moment to moment: that's enough for me, W. says. He supposes it has to be.

If I realised for one moment . . . If I had any real awareness . . . But it would be too much, W. says. I couldn't know what I was, and continue as I am. I couldn't come into any real self-knowledge.

'That's what saves you', W. says. 'Your stupidity'. *If only he knew* . . . : That's what everyone thinks when they see me, W. says. That's what *he* thinks.

Meanwhile, it's left to him to bear *the terrible fact of my existence*, W. says. It's *his* problem, not *mine* as it should be, W. says. Everyone blames him for me. —'What's he doing here?', they ask. 'Why did you bring him?' He has to find all the excuses, W. says. He has to be sorry in my place.

Our *eighth* Dogma presentation, our first overseas, we gave drunk, hopelessly drunk, and were almost completely incoherent. Only one person attended our *ninth*, so we went to the pub instead. For our *tenth*, we drank steadily through our presentation, cracking open can after can.

The Dogmatist must always be *drunk*, that's the next rule, W. says. Drunk: yes, of course. We used to think drunkenness might come *after* thought, might *follow* a successful presentation, a fruitful discussion. But now we understand that drunkenness *belongs* to thought. In the current madness, close to the end, who can bear the thoughts that must be thought? Who can bear it — the coming end?

You have to drink, we agree. Drink to think; drink to present the results of thought. It's a discipline, we decide. You have to start early and continue, steadily. We owe it to ourselves. No: we owe it to thought!

But for our *eleventh* presentation, we drank too much. W. was sick in the toilets before we started. I was green faced. Green lipped! Never again, he says. It should be a new rule: Dogma is sober. *Especially* sober! No, that's a stupid rule, W. says.

How many rules do we have now?, W. wonders. Dogma

is *collaborative*—he remembers that rule. Dogma is *clear*—did we make that a rule? The presentation must be intelligible to everyone. Anyone must be able to follow its points, its logic. Dogma is fundamentally *democratic*, W. says.

Dogma is *personal*—we've agreed on that before, he says. Use anecdotes! Speak of your life and its intersection with thought! Speak of your friends! Speak of your passions and of your misfortunes!

Dogma is *reticent*—that should be a rule, too, W. says. What is spoken is not for publishing. Scorn publication! Publication is for fools! But then Dogma is *studious*: we need to remember that, W. says. Work hard on your presentation. Read everything. Nothing should be left to the last minute. There must be nothing slapdash!

W. names the next rule: Dogma is *apocalyptic*. Dogma accepts that these are the last days. Catastrophe is impending. Bear this in mind as you speak! You must only speak about *what matters most*!

Dogma is on the side of the suffering, we should remember that, W. says. We should think of the poor. We need to keep the memory of the poor before us at all times. Dogma is *advocative*!, W. says.

What next? Oh yes: Dogma is *peripheral*. It avoids famous names. It is shy of fashionable topics. Dogma stays on the outside, with the people of the outside, W. says. It has nothing to do with the centre! Dogma *eschews* the centre, W. says.

But we mustn't forget: Dogma is *affirmative*. Ignore those with whom you disagree. There's no point! '*Never let the critic teach you the cloth*', W. says, quoting Burroughs.

A final rule, a kind of meta-rule, W. says: Dogma is *experimental*. More rules can be added, but only through the *experience of Dogma*.

We should shoot ourselves, W. says. Or maybe he should shoot me, and I him, in a kind of Mexican standoff. Then we would lie there under the sun, bullets in our heads, flies buzzing around us, and there would be a great rejoicing. But that's just it, isn't it: there would be no rejoicing. No one would see, no one would know what the world had been delivered from.

How is it that we've escaped detection?, W. wonders. How is it we've got away with what we have? It would restore faith in the world if we were hunted down and shot. At the last moment, the gun held to our temples, we would laugh in gladness because we would know that justice had been done. It would all make sense! The world would be restored!

That we're still alive, W. says, is a sign of the nearness of the end.

Zeno of Citium strangled himself, W. says. Imagine! He was already an old man by then, and felt he'd missed his appointment with death. Why had it overlooked him? Very well, he would bring death to himself. He would make his own appointment with the end.

And what about us? Should we strangle ourselves? Should I strangle W., and W. me? But that's just it: death doesn't want us, W. says.

If we die, it will be from some stupid accident, the most absurd of illnesses, an ingrowing toenail, for example. It will not be a matter of integrity, or an act of martyrdom. We'll die for nothing, for no purpose. How could we *presume* to take our own lives?

Loving is stronger than death, muses W. —'What do you think that means? Do you have any idea?' For Rosenzweig, W. explains, with love you leave behind the natural order, the boundaries of self and ego. *Immanence is broken*: that's what it means to love. Love is stronger than death, stronger than solitude, stronger than autonomy: that's what Rosenzweig says, it's very moving.

Are we capable of love?, W. muses. Is he? Am I? —'Have you ever been in love with anyone, I mean, really in love?' W. doubts it. I read too many gossip magazines, for one thing. Love's not based on fantasy, as I seem to think. It's an ethical act. —'But you're not capable of that, are you?' I'm fundamentally a *fantasiser*, says W., and know nothing about the living reality of other human beings.

Broken immanence. Wouldn't that be an altogether better

name for our intellectual movement? Or for an '80s style band, like Flock of Seagulls, W. says.

'*The crisis consists precisely in the fact that the old is dying and the new cannot be born*'. W. is reading from his notebooks. '*In this interregnum a great variety of morbid symptoms appears*'. That's Gramsci, he says. It's from the *Prison Notebooks*.

Morbid symptoms — is that what we are? Is that our significance? Then we need to see it all the way through, W. says. We have to press towards the new, and all the way to death. We have to *live* the crisis, W. says. We have to *become* the crisis.

Sometimes W. feels like one of the pillar saints, like Simon Stylites in Syria in the first century AD, waiting for the Messiah to return. When's he coming, the anointed one? When will W. be redeemed?

W.'s perched on his pillar, reading his books in the great languages of Europe. He's reading, he's taking notes in the great languages, ancient and modern, and there I am at the base, masturbating in the dust.

Omoi, that's what W. wants to say. Or *oy vey!* Or *yoy!* What sound should you make at the end, to acknowledge the end? *Yoy!* It's all over. *Oy vey!* We're done for. *Omoi, omoi:*

the lament of Antigone and her siblings as their father was taken away. No, that was *popoi. Popoi, popoi, popoi,* they said. —'Are you listening down there?', W. says.

'You're never happier than when you make plans', W. says. 'Why is that?' I like to throw plans out ahead of me, W. notes. I always have. It must be the illusion of control, a game of *fort-da* like that of Freud's grandchild.

But then, too, there's something *wild* about my plans, something hopelessly unrealistic, W. says, which reveals the very opposite of control.

There are never well-thought-out tactics, there is never a careful strategy; I plan like a fugitive, like a maniac on the loose, or a prisoner who's been locked up for twenty years. What can I know of what I am planning for? Won't the future, and the terrible conditions of the future, destroy any plan I could possibly have?

Still, there is a charm to my planning, despite everything, W. says. There's a charm to the special joy I take in making plans, as if each plan were a kind of kite, that's how W. pictures it, trailing far, far into the future. As if each were dancing in a remote but lovely sky.

My plan to learn music theory, for example. To read Sanskrit. To master the fundamentals of economics. How fanciful! How impossible, each one of them, as they danced on the end of the string! Better still, my plans for the pair of us, for W. and I. For great collaborative projects. For whole books, and series of books, written together! For flurries of articles!

What faith I show! In him! In us! In the many things we can supposedly accomplish together! Of course, it's all for nothing, W. says. He knows it and I should know it. Indeed, I *do* know it. Only, something in me also knows otherwise. Something remains in me of an unthwarted faith, and this is the key to my charm.

There's no evidence of the rats today, I tell W. on the phone. No digging in the plant pots, no fresh droppings. And no sight of them plunging into the drain, or poking their noses from the black wooden casing built around the pipes in the corner of the yard.

You can hear them at night, I tell W., when the TV is turned off and there's no music on the stereo. You can hear a kind of background noise, a kind of pattering, as of tiny paws on mud. And scratching, eternal scratching, under the floorboards and, it seems, in the walls, within the very walls themselves . . .

I have a kind of awe for the rats, he can tell, W. says. They *impress* me. I approve of them. They seem to be *on my side*.

W. remembers reading about a Hindu temple dedicated to rats. —'It was sacred to a mystic. Karni something'. Karani Mata, I tell him. An avatar of the Goddess. —'The rats were supposed to be incarnations of her descendants or something', W. says. 'Anyway, the article showed pictures of thousands of rats, swarming all over the temple. Rats everywhere!'

The rats of the temple, W. says, have got no natural

predators, so they're as friendly as anything, W. says. The pilgrims bring them food to eat—sweet things, mostly, but also vegetable curry—and leave out dishes of milk. It's supposed to be good luck when the rats stream over your feet, he says. It's good fortune to nibble what they've nibbled, and sip what they've drunk.

Yes, even he was moved by the sight of the rats, basking on the bronze mesh that serves as a kind of roof to the temple (it's supposed to keep birds of prey away), and scampering along the rat-runs the temple builders worked into the floor. They'll climb up visitors as up walking trees, W. says. They'll climb, and if you hurt them, you have to give the temple a statue of a rat made of pure gold.

Is that what it was like in the Age of Gold?, we wonder. Is that what it was like for all creatures, basking together in the sun? And will that time come again, when humankind and its brother and sister creatures will each be an image of the Goddess?

Is that what's going to happen to my flat?, W. wonders. Will it become a Hindu temple?

Plymouth. Dinner time. W. is a systematic cook. On weekend mornings, he goes through his *Sainsbury's* magazines deciding what to cook that evening. Then he goes to the supermarket to buy his ingredients, before preparing dinner with meticulousness and love.

He loves to cook, W. says, and enjoys anticipating a good meal. He savours his anticipation. He's not like me, W. says, who eats only discount sandwiches that go cheap after their sell-by date. He doesn't march round Eldon Square just before closing time in search of a bargain sandwich or a box of salad for 75p.

W. knows the value of deferred gratification, he says, which I do not. —'As soon as you feel any pang of hunger, you have to feed yourself', W. notes. In fact, W. is not sure I've ever felt a pang of hunger. —'It's an addiction with you, isn't it? If you don't eat every hour on the hour, you get panicky. You have to have something in your mouth'.

He can see I'm hungry, W. says. —'Go on, go and get a slab of beer. Go and get your pork scratchings'.

We speak of our absent friends, over beers. Where are they now? Scattered all over the world! If only they were closer! Of what would we be capable? They would make us great!

Perhaps that is his last temptation, W. says, the thought that something could make us great.

When did it begin, W.'s exalted view of friendship? When did he receive his great vision of comradeship? At his grandmother's caravan park, he says, as a child. His parents sent him there every summer. He would stay for weeks at a time, playing in the fields by the sea.

It reminded W. of the Canadian wilderness that he had left behind. It reminded him of what he had lost: the breadth of the sky, the virgin earth, and whole days of wandering, with no parents to supervise him. Children should be brought up with *benign neglect*: isn't that what W. has always maintained?

W. made a friend at the caravan park, a friend of the kind you might make in Canada, W. says. A *working class* friend, like me. Except utterly unlike me, because his friend had a sense of loyalty. His friend knew nothing of betrayal! Nothing of treachery!

Open space is good for friendship, W. says. Friendship needs expanses, he says. It needs to fill its lungs. His friend and he looked for adders in the woods, and toads in the marshland at the edge of the dunes. They trespassed on farmland, too, smoking among the hay-bales.

They were chased by farmers, and ran back to the caravan

park through the fields. Once, they saw a police car, pulling up the park drive, and knew they were in trouble.

But there was no betrayal. When one stumbled, the other helped him up. When one fell, the other carried him. When one was accused, the other would take the blame . . . It was like *Spartacus*, W. says. The *cadre* was everything. The collective. And hasn't that been what he's sought ever since?

If there were a few more of us . . . , W. says. A few more, living close to us, helping one another think. Helping us, even us. If I lived closer, W. says, instead of hundreds of miles away, something might be possible. We're islands, he says, stranded at opposite ends of the country.

W. dreams, like Phaedrus, of an army of thinker-friends, thinker-lovers. He dreams of a thought-army, a thought-pack, which would storm the philosophical Houses of Parliament. He dreams of Tartars from the philosophical steppes, of thought-barbarians, thought-outsiders. What distances would shine in their eyes!

Sal is always moved by my response to dinner. A cooked meal! I'm amazed. A whole chicken, steaming on the table! I become quite delirious. I can barely contain my excitement. It's as if I've never eaten before. She can only *imagine* what kind of life I usually lead.

Sal refuses to visit my flat, of course. It's too squalid. The plaster dust. The slugs. And there's rubble in the shower. How do I wash? *Do* I wash? And there's no food. Nothing. I can't have food in my house, I've told them, because I eat it all. I binge. I stuff myself. I make myself ill almost immediately. So there's no food.

Then, too, I've no fridge, and nowhere to store food. There's no electricity in the kitchen, and besides, it's dismantled, ready for another round of damp-proofing. The walls are so wet! It's like touching the skin of a frog—clammy.

Sal can imagine a terrible plague spreading from the flat. A new kind of illness, which travels by damp spores. And the flat's so dark! It's like being buried underground, staying at the flat, she says. It's like being buried alive. —'And you haven't told her about the rats yet', W. says.

W. remembers the worst, he says. He remembers the green dressing gown with its great holes. He remembers the stretches of white flesh which showed through those holes. —'Your rolls of fat', says W.

It was like the story of Noah over again, when Shem saw his father naked. He might as well have seen *me* naked, W. says, and shudders. Actually, that would have been better. But the green dressing gown, with its holes . . . It was the worst of sights, W. says. The very worst.

'Compare this house to your flat', W. says. 'How high are your ceilings? As high as these?' W.'s ceilings are fifteen feet high. No, they're not that high, I tell him. My flat's tiny, which he knows full well. —'How *dry* is your flat?', W. says, knowing the answer. It's not dry at all, I tell him. His house is as *dry as a bone*, W. tells me. It couldn't be drier. And of course, W.'s house is rat-free, he tells me.

'Do you think you've failed?', W. says. And then, 'Was buying your flat the *outcome* of your failure, or did it merely *complete* your failure?'

Why did I buy my flat? What led me to it? W. wants to be taken through the decision-making process step by step, he says. And I really had no idea about the damp when I viewed it? My surveyors didn't tell me about the underground river? My bank didn't withhold my loan when they heard that it was built on top of a mineshaft, and was collapsing in the middle?

It's where I thought I *deserved* to live, W. says. It's what

I thought I *warranted*. W., of course, ended up in a three sto-
rey Georgian townhouse. He's still amazed by that. How did
he end up with this kind of house, and a lecturing job, and a
woman who loves him?

Ah, but these are his last days in his house, he's certain
of it. These are his last days in his job. And are these his
last days with Sal, too? She would never leave him, W. says.
Surely, she would never leave him . . .

His last days . . . he feels it in the air, as animals sense
a storm. It's building up out there, W. says, it's massing like
storm clouds over Plymouth Sound.

'Take some photos', W. says. 'It needs to be documented!'
I photograph the wide entrance hall and the stairs to the
next floor. I photograph the ground floor living room, with
internal shutters over the window and a marble fireplace. I
photograph the CDs lined up alphabetically on the shelf, and
the pile of CDs without covers by the ghetto blaster.

I photograph full ashtrays and discarded Emmenthal
packets. I photograph the great kitchen where sometimes we
dance, sliding on our socks, and the tiny toilet on the ground
floor, with pictures of their friends on the wall. Why haven't
they got a picture of me?, I ask them. No reply.

Upstairs, I document the great living room in a series of
photos which, laid edge to edge, would give the whole pan-
orama: the wide floorboards and the high, old skirting; the
tall windows, newly restored; the king-sized fireplace, with its
resplendent tiles and marble surround . . .

It's here we come to listen to Jandek, W. and I, sitting on the couch with great seriousness. I make him listen in silence to *Khartoum* and *Khartoum Variations*. W. finds Jandek very disturbing, and needs me in the room to listen to the music with him. Sal never stays for Jandek. —'I hate fucking Jandek', she says. 'Don't play Jandek while I'm in the house', she says.

I document the great bathroom, too—the greatest of bathrooms, we're all agreed. The lion-footed bath on a raised plinth. The fulsomeness of the airing cupboard, with its many towels, sheets and duvet covers. The pile of *Uncuts* by the toilet, ready to read. The stained glass window, made by someone famous.

Ah, how will he leave it, his house?, W. says. He'll have to leave it, he knows that. They'll sack him. They'll drive him out of his city. It's coming, the end is coming.

Up another flight to the top floor, and the holy of holies: W.'s study. His bookshelves—not too many, since W. gives away most of his books ('I don't hoard them, like you', he says), but enough for all the essentials. His Hebrew/English dictionary. His volumes of Cohen. His collected Rosenzweigs.

This is the room where I sleep when I stay. W. pulls out a camp bed and makes it up. He has to fumigate his study after I've slept in it, he says. It has to be re-consecrated, his temple of scholarship.

Then, finally, W.'s and Sal's room, calm, generous and large-windowed. This is where he recovers from his days of scholarship, W. says. And it's where he wakes up, before dawn, ready for his studies.

W.'s still reading Rosenzweig, very slowly, in German, every morning, he tells me. —'I don't understand a word'. Still, it's a good exercise. Every morning, he goes into his study and sits at his desk before he does anything else. Does he have a cup of tea? No, he says, tea has to wait. How about coffee? He doesn't have coffee, either. I always begin with a cup of coffee, I tell him. —'That's where you go wrong', he says. 'Some things take precedence over coffee'.

How does he dress himself for scholarship?, I ask him. He wears his dressing gown, W. says. He sits in his dressing gown and reads, looking up difficult German words (which is to say, most of them) in his dictionary. How does he do it?, he wonders. Every morning, he leaves Sal lying there in the warm bed, and goes to work. Is she impressed by his commitment? —'She thinks I'm an idiot', W. says.

We admire W.'s edition of the collected Rosenzweig. —'What you have to understand is that Rosenzweig was very, very clever', he says. 'We'll never, whatever we do, be as clever as him. We'll never have a single idea, and he had hundreds of ideas'.

W.'s workfiles mean little to him now, he says. There are dozens of them, saved in a folder called *Notes*, on every kind of topic. Spinoza's *Theologico-Political Treatise*, for example. Hermann Cohen's *Religion of Reason*. He saves them to his folder and forgets them immediately, W. says. Why does he bother?

I open one on his computer screen. Notes from Cohen's

Mathematics and the Theory of Platonic Ideas, long out of print. It cost him £130, he sighs. W. makes himself read things by spending very large amounts of money on them. He feels so guilty, he *has* to read them. Cohen's *The Principle of the Method of Infinitesimals and its History* — that cost him £210!

But what would I know of all this?, W. says. My reading is done online. I barely know what it means to *handle a volume.* And besides, old books, with their learning, frighten me, he knows that. Old hardbacks with scholarly footnotes. Old libraries — what do I know of them? I'm a man of the *new age,* W. says, just as he is a man of the *old age.* He's an anachronism, W. says, he knows that; and I am a harbinger.

Stonehouse, morning. —'You should always live among the poor', W. says, as we thread through the crowd of refugees gathered at the end of the road. They're always standing about outside, the sun on their faces, W. says. He likes that. They're *men of the street*, as he is. But where are their womenfolk? Where do they live? It's a mystery to him, W. says.

We're heading to the sea. That's what Plymouth means to him, W. says: proximity to the sea. He has to see it!, W. says. He has to be near it! It's as essential to him as oxygen. He is a *scholar of the coast*, W. says, which means he's bound to end up living inland, far inland, when he loses his job. He's a *scholar of fresh air*, which means he'll end up living somewhere underground and fetid, just like me, W. says.

On the road by the Hoe, the council have stuck little metal pillars into the road, with the names of famous former residents written on them. What traces will we leave? What will be our immortality?

We pay to enter Smeaton Tower, the old lighthouse, and ascend its winding staircase. The lighthouse was moved from the breakwater, W. says when we reach the top. It's only ornamental now; the real lighthouse is much further out to sea. We squint out over the waves. Yes, there it is, in the far distance.

W. takes me to his favourite café, to see if we can find the young Polish woman who used to serve us. He wants me to have a *romantic interest*, W. says. He wants to see me stutter and fumble. He wants to see me pucker my lips for a kiss. But she isn't there, and he has to listen to my *caffeine theories* instead, as he drinks his coffee.

'You'll have to document all this', W. says, as we walk through the shopping arcades. I need to document his *Plymouth years*, W. says. He takes me on a *pointing tour* of his favourite buildings.

I take photos of W. pointing to particular architectural features he admires. He points to the high brown façade of the new university arts building. He points to the decrepit Palace Theatre. He tells me again how the old city was razed by the Luftwaffe, and how it was rebuilt in the '50s, following the Abercrombie Plan. .

I take a picture of him pointing directly up into the sky, from where the Luftwaffe came, and then, standing on a bench, pointing directly at the earth, where the bombs struck. I ask a passerby to take a photo of W. pointing at me, and of me pointing at W., and finally of W. and I pointing at one another.

The Plymouth Gin cocktail bar. My working class credentials are far better than his, W. says over our Martinis. He is invariably moved when he thinks of me leaving school and working in the warehouse, and feels a great urge to protect and encourage me. —'How long were you there?', he asks me, and when I tell him, he gasps. —'That long!' And then, 'What did you do there?', and when I tell him, he gasps again.

'What was your job title?', W. always asks me. I was a *Transactions Analyst*, I tell him. 'And what were your duties?' I looked for UTLs, Unable-To-Locates. I checked van manifests and loading bays, looking for missing items. I searched high and low in the racks on my order picker. I quizzed fellow workers about their procedures and made reports to management about how many boxes had been lost and how warehouse procedures might be streamlined.

'You were so keen at first!', says W. He can see me, in his mind's eye, with my overalls and toetectors. He sees my willing stupidity, my sense of *wanting to do well* and of the British Standards I was brought in to enforce.

But my mouth began to twitch, didn't it? My eyes began to focus, not on the job at hand, the item I was looking for, but on the middle distance. I grew a beard and looked like a Tartar. He sees me, W. says, wandering back to the station after work, with a vague sense that something was missing in my life.

And from then on, when I found them, my missing items, I only hid them more deeply, didn't I? W. says. I threw my unable-to-locates into obscure cupboards. I buried them in the racks. I neglected my paperwork. My reports were less artful. My British Standards manuals went unread.

'That's when you began to read, isn't it?', W. says. This is his favourite part of the story. There was a flight of stairs that led up to the roof, which no one ever used. That's where I went to read in my lunch hour. It's where I began to work my way through the books I found in the library.

What was the book I started with?, he asks. Oh yes: *The Mammoth Book of Fantasy*, he could never forget that. I began with *The Mammoth Book of Fantasy*, W. says, and read my way up to Kafka. 'You put down *The Mammoth Book of Fantasy*, and picked up *The Castle*', W. remembers. 'That's when it began, isn't it?'

W. finds it very poignant, he says. I might have spent the rest of my life reading *The Mammoth Book of Fantasy*, and books like *The Mammoth Book of Fantasy*, but there I was with my Kafka.

W. *began* with Kafka, of course, he says. He remembers it very clearly, his first encounter with the Schocken editions of Kafka in his school library ('We *had* a school library', he says, 'unlike you'). They had orange dustcovers, W. says. Why he was attracted by that colour, he'll never know. But there it was: *The Castle*.

The Castle, W. says. He didn't have to mouth those letters to himself to understand them, W. says. He could actually read, unlike me. He didn't have to wrinkle his brow and mouth the letters out loud.

But still, says W., he remains infinitely moved by the mental image of me sitting on the stairs that led up to the roof, *The Mammoth Book of Fantasy* already long behind me. He remains immeasurably moved by the image of the

ape-child who sat on the stairs, mouthing the letters *T-H-E-*
-C-A-S-T-L-E to himself.

W. is overwhelmed by work, he says. Broken by it, by the prospect of it. Administration! I love it, of course. I'm at it all day in my office. How do I even begin?, W. wonders. How can I make a start when the task itself is so immense?

I must not be able to see the whole thing, W. says. The big picture is closed to me. Otherwise, how could I go on? How could I persist from day to day? W., by comparison, is a seer, he says. He's seen too much! He knows where it's heading! He's seen through the day to the night, and to the night of all nights.

He can imagine it, W. says: I pause from my ceaseless administrative work, look up for a moment . . . What am I thinking about? What thought has struck me? But he knows I am full only of *administrative anxieties*, and my pause is only a slackening of the same relentless movement.

And what of him, when he looks up from his administrative labours? What does he see? Of what is he dreaming? Of a single thought from which something might begin, he says. Of a single thought that might justify his existence.

W.'s college has become a *vale of tears*, he says. It's a bit like *Werckmeister Harmonies*, after the arrival of the whale, W.

says. Chaos everywhere. Petty vandalism. Dead bodies, face down in the quadrangle, with knives in their backs.

It'll go up in flames, soon, the college, W. says. There'll be black smoke rising from the lecture halls. And after that, who knows? Cannibalism, probably. Human sacrifice.

What would I do in his situation?, W. asks. What's the *Hindu solution*? Oh, he remembers my advice: he should apply for that job in the Lebanon, I told W. That lectureship in philosophy in Beirut. He's not going to Beirut, W. says. Forget it. People are kidnapped in Beirut! They end up in solitary confinement for years and years! Actually, he'd make quite a good hostage, W. says. He would sit in his manacles in the dark, thinking about the Stoics . . .

He should go straight to the Lebanon, and become a scholar of Arabic, I told him. —'Oh yes, is that what you'd do?', he asked me. He should become a scholar of Averroes, I told him, and write on the board from right to left. He's not going to become a scholar of Averroes, W. says.

He should apply for work in Zambia or Botswana, I told W. He should apply to become Lecturer in Philosophy at Lusaka University. They're too far away!, W. says. Too hot! Would *I* apply for a job in Zambia or Botswana?, he says. 'Of course not'. Zambia and Botswana are out for him too, W. says. No, if we get sacked, he's going to come to live in my flat, W. says. He'll bring Sal. I'll have to go to work in Zambia or Botswana, and support them.

Our friends, what has happened to our friends?, W. wonders.

Are the rumours true? Have they really broken into war-
ring factions? Are there really Facebook groups, dedicated to
mutual destruction?

A war among friends: can I conceive of anything more
terrible?, W. says. Who started it? Whose fault is it? Ah, but
he knows the cause, W. says: cynicism. Opportunism. He
knows how it began. It always begins the same way!

Cynicism, opportunism. This is the time of the rat, W.
says. A time without justice, without goodness. A time without God!

To think it could even reach our friends, W. says. To
think that even *they* could be infected . . .

W.'s dream has always been that we might save ourselves
from the end, he and I. But we won't be able to hold it back,
he knows that now. The disaster strikes first at what is closest
to us, W. says.

And what's my role in all this?, W. wonders. Where do I
stand? *Et tu*?, W. will say as I slip the knife between his ribs.
Et tu, idiot?

How many times have I betrayed him?, W. wonders. I'm
on every page of his Book of Betrayals. He's always taken
detailed notes. And there are pictures, too. W. wants to
remember everything. Everything!

One day, he's going to read his notes to me and show
me all his pictures, he says. One day, standing at the head of
the bed like the Archangel Michael, he's going to read me the
great list of my betrayals and show me the pictures.

I think the rats are losing their fear of me, I tell W. on the phone. They're out in the open now, in the yard, bathing in the drain.

I should stop playing Jandek, W. says. It summons them out of their lairs. I'm like the pied piper of Spital Tongues, W. says.

W.'s decline is getting worse, he says. He's sure that the very capacity to think is retreating from him. He's losing them one by one, his intellectual faculties, the organs of thought . . .

Species trapped on islands undergo changes in scale, W. says. They can become large — grotesquely large in the case of giant tortoises and komodo dragons. Or they can become small, minaturising over the generations, W. says, like that species of tiny people whose remains were discovered on that remote island. What were they called?

They shared their island with pygmy elephants and giant rats, W. says. They hunted rats on the backs of pygmy elephants, or pygmy elephants on the backs of rats, one of the two. —'They had great flat feet like yours', W. says, 'and an improbably small brain, no doubt like yours'. And they murmured rather than spoke. And they whistled and hooted, just as I am a whistler and hooter.

Homo Floresiensis, that's it! I've become a *Homo Floresiensis of thought*, W. says. It's terrible. Didn't I used to appear intelligent? Even W. is forgetting. That's how it seemed, he says, improbable as it sounds. And now?

It's my flat, W. says. The squalor of my flat. It's the squalor of my life, my isolation, which is the equivalent of the island of Flores. But haven't I become *larger* rather than smaller? I'm like one of those giant rats, W. says. He's going to climb on a pigmy elephant and hunt me down.

W. fears he's also becoming a *Homo Floresiensis of thought*. Isn't he becoming shorter by the day? Aren't his feet getting bigger and flatter? Isn't his brainpan shrinking and his chin looking a little more sloped?

He's following my example, W. says. He's declining. He's beginning to forget the higher ideas. Good God, he can barely count! He can barely add two numbers together! Is this what happened on the island of Flores? Is this where our collaboration has led him?

'No one can benefit from redemption / That star stands far too high. / And if you had arrived there too, / You would still stand in your own way'. W. is reading from Scholem's didactic poem.

'How do you think it applies to you?', W. says. 'Do you get in your own way?' I get in *his* way, that's for sure, W. says. And perhaps, in my company, something in *him* also gets in his way.

It's my fault, he's sure of that, W. says. If I weren't around, he might reach the star of redemption . . . But perhaps I exist only as a materialisation of his sin, W. says. Perhaps *Lars* is a name for his own failure. Perhaps I am only that part of himself that stands in his way . . .

Retrospective redemption, that's what W. is holding out for. It *will have made sense*, he says. It will always have made sense from the perspective of redemption, that's what he hopes. But there's little sign of it, he concedes. In fact, it's getting worse.

He hears the dull rumble of thunder, W. says. The storm is coming; lightning could flash down at any time. But why does no one else hear it? Why does no one but him know the signs? Make it stop!, W. wants to cry—but to whom? *Make it stop!*—but not to me, since I am only part of the catastrophe, only a catastrophic scrap torn off to torment him.

W. sends me a quotation from Simone Weil:

> *The proper method of philosophy consists in clearly conceiving the insoluble problems in all their insolubility and then in simply contemplating them, fixedly and tirelessly, year after year, patiently waiting.*

W.'s proper method of philosophy, he says, consists in clearly conceiving the insoluble problem of my stupidity in all its insolubility and then in simply contemplating it, fixedly and tirelessly, year after year, patiently waiting . . .

Ah, but perhaps that's his stupidity, W. says: believing that I could ever leave my stupidity behind.

The *argumentum ad misericordiam*, that's the name for it, W. says, my basic scholarly move. It's the fallacy of appealing to pity or sympathy, which in my case is implied in the *state* of the speaker: my bloodshot eyes, my general decay. Don't I always give my presentations as though *on my knees?*, W. says.

It's as though I'm praying for mercy, W. says, although it's also, no doubt, a plea to put me out of my misery. *Kill me now*, that's what my presentations say. *Don't spare me.* Which is why, inevitably, I am spared. It would be too easy to destroy me, W. says. And who would clean up afterwards?

He's tried to put me out of my misery, W. says. God knows, he's tried. Hasn't everyone? No one had tried hard enough, that's what W. discerned when we first met. And it became his task, to try hard enough. And what a task! How many times has he tried? How many emails has he sent?

But it won't get through, W. says. I won't hear him. He's resorted to blows, W. says, but it's like beating a big, dumb animal. It seems pointless and cruel. How can I understand why I am being beaten? I bellow, that's all. It's perfectly senseless to me.

He's drawn pictures, W. says. He's scrawled red lines across my work, but I have never understood; I've carried on regardless.

No!. he writes in the margin. *Rubbish!*, he writes, underscoring the word several times, his biro piercing the paper. But still I continue. Still I go on, one page after another.

Rat poison works by *thinning the blood*, that's what the pest controller said, I tell W. on the phone. It's an anticoagulant, which means the rats will bleed to death from the smallest of cuts. They'll bleed internally, too. It's a terrible way to die. I'll hear them screeching in pain and horror, I tell W.

The controller told me to smash some glass around the nest. That way, the rats will cut themselves on the shards and bleed to death, their wounds prevented from healing.

Imagine it: rats bleeding inside, their organs compressed all the way to failure. Rats, organs torn, their blood escaped from circulation and pooling inside their bodies. Rats with dark red blood streaming from their arteries and veins . . .

What a terrible way to die! What a terrible way *not to be able to die!* Because as they run, streaming, screeching in horror, they'll want only for their lives to end, for their pain to end. What else will they want but for death to finish with them, for the blood to ooze from their capillaries?

That's how we'll die, like rats, W. says. Like rats, running along with everyone else, screeching. The flaming sky, the sun come close, and rats like us streaming, screeching across the baking earth . . .

When will it end?, I ask W. —'It will never end', he says. When will it stop?, I ask him. —'It will never stop'.

Teacakes at a café on the Hoe. A blue-grey destroyer sits flush from us in the harbour, and smaller vessels go back and forth.

The Navy's pulling out of Plymouth, W. tells me. Five hundred years they've been here. They're moving operations up to Scotland. Plymouth's finished, of course, W. says. It's all over.

We take a tour of the dockyards, heading up though Devonport on the Tamar. The largest naval site in Europe, W. says. But soon it will all be gone, he says of the shipyards and the tidal berths, the factories and the dry-docks. They'll pull it all down. It'll be as though it was never there. The same will happen when *he*'s expelled from the city, W. says. They'll pull down *his* house and destroy *his* things, W. says.

They're going to sack him, he's sure of it. They're going to force him out. And when they force him from his job, they'll force him out of Plymouth. What work will he find in Plymouth, after he's sacked? None. There's nothing for him here. There's nothing for any of them, any of his colleagues, most of whom have already left.

Plymouth minus W., W. minus Plymouth . . . A man without a city is a terrible thing, W. says. He wonders what I would be without my city. He sees me, in his mind's eye:

expelled, wandering across the earth. And he sees himself beside me, pushing our shopping cart full of Plymouth Gin through the gathering darkness . . .

W. tells me of his months as an artist's model, being painted by Robert Lenkiewicz, the Plymouth Rembrandt. Lenkiewicz only wanted to talk about philosophy, W. says. He was obsessed with philosophy. He bankrupted himself buying philosophy books, W. says.

Lenkiewicz bought a derelict church and filled it with books, piles and piles of them, it was quite extraordinary, W. says. W. would look through the mouldering books with Lenkiewicz, and the painter would pick up a volume here and there to show him. Lenkiewicz had Maimonides's *Treatise on Logic* in the first English edition. He had Nicholas of Cusa's *Of Learned Ignorance*. He had the page-proofs of Blanchot's *The Step Not Beyond*, worth thousands of pounds.

Lenkiewicz was painting W. in a series of works called *Obsession*, W. tells me. He always painted in series, Lenkiewicz — *projects*, he called them. He had a *Vagrancy* project and a *Street Drinking* project. He had a *Mentally Handicapped* project. But W. was part of the *Obsession* project, or he was supposed to be. Lenkiewicz died very suddenly, just like that, and it was all over. They had to sell all his paintings to meet his debts. They sold his books too — they had to sell the whole church full of books . . .

'Do you think Lenkiewicz would have painted you?', W. says. 'Do you think he would have stuck you in one of his portraits?' W. can see it now, he says, Lenkiewicz's *Study for a Moron*, part of his *Idiocy* project. Lenkiewicz's *Orang-Utan of Thought*, part of his *Philosophical Apes* project . . .

Lenkiewicz was going to paint the whole philosophy and theology department of his college, W. says. He was going to execute one of his epic works, modelled on Géricault or something. He can see it in his mind's eye, W. says: Lenkiewicz's own *Raft of the Medusa*, heaving with crazed and starving members of the philosophy and theology department . . .

Ah, but what's going to happen to it now, the philosophy and theology department? It's going to be closed, W. says. It will be closed, and its members set adrift, W. says. Who among them will survive, after the *wreck of the humanities*?

A visit to my hometown. To my home *suburbs*, W. says. He wants to know where it all went wrong. —'You started well enough, didn't you? You had advantages in life. You weren't starving. You weren't brought up in a war zone . . . ' When did it go wrong?, W. asks. *Where* did it go wrong?

He sees it immediately. Houses jammed together. Cars packing the driveways. There's no *expanse*!, W. says. There are no *vistas*! Every single bit of land is accounted for. Everything is owned, used, put to work . . .

This is the way the world will end: as a gigantic suburb, that's what W. used to think, he says. But now he knows the world will end in the skies *above* the suburbs. That's where they'll ride, the four horsemen of our apocalypse.

These are the days, W. says. This is the reckoning. Of what though? He's unsure. There must be some kind of accounting, he knows that. Someone must be keeping score, but who?

Sometimes, W. thinks I'm glad I live in the End Times. Isn't the coming apocalypse the perfect correlate of my desire for ruination? Isn't the destruction of the world only the macrocosmic version of my self-destruction? What would I be without the End? A man whose madness signified nothing, spoke of nothing. A symptom without a disease . . .

It's different with him, of course. He was made for the beginning of the world, not the end of it. He is a man of *hope*, W. says. Of the youth of the world. Ah, but that's not true, not really, he grants. He is a man of the end who yearns for the beginning, yearns for innocence, as I do not. He looks back, into the vanished glory of the past, and I look forward, into the storm clouds of catastrophe.

W. has grown increasingly convinced that intellectual conversation itself is an affectation, he says, as we head out for our walk. At first, he had supposed it was bad manners to talk of abstract things at dinner. When you eat, eat, that's what he had thought, and save the abstract matters for later.

But now? Intellectual conversation — so-called intellectual conversation — is inappropriate at any time, W. says. It's a ruse. An excuse. We have to plunge into concrete matters, W. says. Our conversation must be as concrete as our eating.

'This wood, for example. That field. And that — what is that?' A barrow, I tell him. An ancient burial mound. But W. says that it's only a refuse heap. A pile of rubbish abandoned among the trees.

He can imagine me as a boy, W. says, cycling out through the new housing estates, and through what remained of the woodland — muddy tracks along field-edges, fenced-in bridleways and overgrown footpaths. — 'You were looking for something', he says. 'You knew something was missing'.

He sees it in his mind's eye: I'm carrying my bike over the railway bridge. I'm cycling through glades of tree stumps in the forestry plantations. I'm following private roads past posh schools and riding academies. I'm looking for barrows and ley lines, W. says. I'm looking for Celtic gods and gods of any kind.

And what do I find as I wheel my bike across the golf course? What, in the carpark of an out of town retail park? What, on the bench outside the supermarket, eating my discounted sandwiches? The *everyday*, W. says, which is to say, the opposite of the gods.

At the company where I used to work, I tell W., they named their meeting rooms after philosophers. You could book *Locke* for a meeting, or *Kant*, or *Wittgenstein*. —'Did they have a Diogenes room?', W. asks. 'A Diogenes barrel?'

At lunchtimes, I would photocopy pages from library books by Kafka, I tell him. The *Octavo Notebooks*. Bits from the diaries and letters. I'd keep them in a folder in my drawer, hidden, I tell him. I was like a fairytale giant, burying his heart in a treasure chest at the bottom of a lake.

In the folder was my heart, or so I thought, I tell W. Kafka was the *very opposite* of Hewlett Packard. Kafka, my heart, was the *very opposite* of Bracknell. But what, in the end, could I understand of Kafka? What could the *Octavo Notebooks* mean to me as I looked out towards the massive hotel at the roundabout, built in the style of a Swiss mountain chalet?

I wandered all day through the company corridors. I drifted from coffee machine to coffee machine. I stared off through the windows. I sat on the leather sofas in the foyer and read trade magazines at lunchtime. And what did I see? What did I know?

Through the golf course. We wait on the path while a golfer hits his ball into the distance. He starts to yell. —'Oy, leave it alone!' Four lads, sauntering onto the fairway, have pocketed the ball. The golfer shouts again. —'That's my ball!'

'*That is my place in the sun*', W. quotes from Pascal. '*Here is the beginning and prototype of the usurpation of the whole earth . . .*'

4X4s and Land Rovers lined up by the clubhouse. Golfers in their windshirts and their soft-spiked shoes. The enemy, W. says.

'They stole it from us, all this', W. says, looking back over the stream which runs through the golf course, and the footpath which follows its course. 'It was part of the commonwealth, part of the open land we all shared', he says.

I've read Karl Polyani, W. says. I should know the argument: Capitalism began with the enclosure of land. It began as land was seized by the rich and the powerful.

But for W., capitalism began long before that, he says. He evokes the virgin country which revealed itself as the ice sheet retreated, its shorelines stretching far out from where they lie now, joining our country to Europe, to continental Europe.

The climate was warming, W. says. The tundra turned into steppe, and then scrub, and then forest. And in the forests that covered the country, juniper gave way to birch and hazel, and then to oak and elm. Reindeer thrived in the open spaces for a time, and wild horses. Wolves crossed the land-bridge with aurochs and polecats.

Human beings came, W. says, hunter-gatherers, moving nomadically through the landscape. Game was plenty. There were berries and nuts and fruit to gather. They lived from the land, foraging and gleaning . . .

W. dreams of hunters, basking in the sun. He dreams of gatherers, bathing in a plunge pool. He dreams of feasts in the open air. He dreams of cave paintings in the womb of the earth.

There were no leaders back then, W. says. No hierarchies, no bureaucrats. And there was no surplus of resources for particular individuals to horde, either. They shared everything.

The Paleolithic was a lot like Canada, W. says.

What next? W. shakes his head. No, he won't talk about it again, he says. He can't bear it. And then, 'Agriculture', he says. 'The domestication of livestock'.

How long was it before market forces triumphed?, W. wonders. How long before competitiveness did away with friendship and community? Ah, it was a short step to money, the commodity, and the market, W. says. A short step to when capitalism subsumed almost every detail of our lives . . .

And it ends up here, in the suburbs, W. says. It ends up here, on the golf course in the suburbs . . .

Perhaps we've already had our idea, our great chance, W. says, as we climb up the hill towards the church. Perhaps it's already occurred to us, and we've forgotten it: what a terrible thought! Worse still, perhaps it was something we exchanged in conversation, something that passed between us and was immediately lost amidst the general inanity.

That must be my task, W. tells me: remember everything! Write it down!, and perhaps then something will shine forth through the pages like a watermark.

Religion is about *this* world, about the ordinary, the everyday, W. says, over our pints at *The Queen's Oak*. Why does no one understand that but him?, W. says. Why will no one listen?

But when it comes to the everyday itself, I am the expert, not him, W. says. Only I understand what it means to reach the *depths*, which is to say the *surface,* of the everyday?

It has to be *felt*, the everyday, W. is convinced of that. It has to have defeated you. Humiliated you. A man who hasn't been brought to his knees by the everyday can have no understanding of the everyday, says W., aphoristically.

I've certainly been brought to my knees, W. says, that much is clear. I've spent whole *years* on my knees.

W. wants to hear about my *warehouse years*, he says. He wants to hear about my *years of unemployment*. He never tires of it.

'What did you do all day?', he asks me, and when I shrug, he says, 'Take me through it. Take me through one of your days'. There's no point, I tell him. He'll never understand. —'Did you drink a lot?', W. asks. 'Is that how you got through it?' Sometimes I drank, I tell him. Sometimes I did nothing at all. I looked out of the window, I tell him. I watched the raindrops bead and run down the glass.

But W. can never understand. Imagine if he lost his job, I say. Imagine, his job lost, if Sal left him (Sal would never leave him, W. says), and he was stranded in a room, a single room, for year after year. He would become a kind of cosmonaut, all lines cut, tumbling into space, head over heels. Tumbling, falling further and further away, utterly lost . . .

Of course, he'd have his reading, W. says. And his writing. He'd have his intellectual projects. Couldn't he get down, really get down, to learning mathematics? Couldn't he finally master classical Greek, getting past the aorist, which always defeats him?

He'd soon tire of such tasks, I tell him. They would leave him behind; his project would belong to someone else, living another life. The *infinite wearing away*: that's what W. would have to fear, I tell him.

No more reading and writing, I tell him. Books stranded on a desk, open but with no one to read them. And W. watching raindrops bead and run down the windows . . .

'*We are ferociously religious*', says W., quoting Bataille. Are we? —'Oh yes', W. says, 'especially you. Especially you!' That's why he hangs out with me, W. says, he's sure of it: my *immense religious instinct*, of which I am entirely unaware.

It's all to do with my intimate relationship with the everyday, W. says. It's to do with my years of unemployment and menial work, he says.

When he thinks of religion, he immediately thinks of me working in my warehouse, he says. He thinks of me in the warehouse with no hope in my life.

Only the hopeless can truly understand the everyday, W. says. Only they can approach the everyday *at its level*. And only those who can approach the everyday in such a way are really religious, W. says.

Bar queues. Roadies setting up on the stage. Day one of the festival.

What are the kids listening to?, W. wonders as we sip Plymouth Gin from our water bottles. The kids are gentle. They drink, like us, through the morning and the afternoon, through the evening and the night. They sit on the grass outside their chalets, smoking.

We play them *The Texas-Jerusalem Crossroads*. We tell them about Josh T. Pearson. W. plays them apocalyptic Canadian pop. I play them Jandek. I only listen to Jandek, W. tells them. He admires it in me, that consistency, that obsessiveness.

You have to understand that Jandek plays *non-music*, W. tells the kids. That it has very little to do with music at all. Non-melody, non-competence . . . in each case, the 'non-' is not privative, W. explains. Non-melody is *larger* than melody, he says. Non-competence *comprehends* competence. The universe of non-music is *much, much greater* than the universe of music, he says.

Later, in our chalet, Sal passes out drunk. There she is, slumped by the wall, unconscious, and we are too drunk to get off the bed. We can't cross the room! We can't stand up! How else are we going to reach her?

We play her some Jandek, very loud. It'll reach her reptile brain, we agree. Her reptile brain will react in horror. It does. She opens her eyes. —'You twats', she says. 'Why did you wake me up?'

Sal hates Jandek. —'Fucking Jandek. I hate him', she says. —'Lars loves him', says W. —'Well, he would', says Sal, rolling a cigarette, 'he's a fucking twat'. —'Don't anger the Sal', W. says to me. And then, 'We have to sober up'. We have to sober up! Our leader, Josh T. Pearson, is playing at midnight!

We have to compose ourselves, we tell Sal, because our leader is playing. —'He's not *my* leader', says Sal. And then, 'He'd better not be like fucking Jandek'. We tell her she has to come, but she's too drunk to stand. *We're* too drunk to stand!, we tell her. Look at us!

We need food! We need to metabolise the alcohol. We call out to the kids: Bring us some food! But the kids ignore us. They're gentle, W. says of the kids, but lazy. —'Cook something for us, Sal', W. says. —'Fuck off', Sal says.

Day two. The long afternoon. We've set up camp at a table in the upstairs hall. It's dark, the floor's sticky.

We consider the enigma of Josh T. Pearson as we sip our pints. He's living in Berlin, we've heard, and has no intention of recording anything. He's given up recording! He's dreadfully poor, we've heard. He can only afford to eat one meal a day. And he's an illegal immigrant, which means he can't get benefits. He can't afford dental work.

Josh T. Pearson's beard's getting longer. His hair's getting longer. He's vowed never to cut it, we've heard. Not until *the problem of Africa* is solved. He's an ethical man, W. says. Josh T. Pearson thinks only of the suffering in Africa, that's what he said in interview. It's very impressive, W. says.

Josh T. Pearson is a one man band. He doesn't need his former bandmates, we agree. Not when he can stomp his feet for percussion. Not with his array of effects pedals. He sounds like the Pentecost, we agree.

Last night, he sang of celestial wars, of angels battling demons, of the apocalypse and the end of times. He sang of prophets and messiahs, false and true . . . He sang of the *messianic epoch*, says W. Josh T. Pearson was dreaming of justice. He was dreaming of the redemption of Africa and the redemption of the world.

Josh T. Pearson! Ah, how can we understand what he's become? It's beyond us, we agree. He speaks from inside the burning bush. He speaks from the whirlwind. The battle takes place in his heart. Angels versus devils. Christ versus the Anti-Christ . . .

And who are we, in our festival afternoon? Devils ourselves, W. says. Anti-Christs ourselves . . . Ah, when will Josh T. Pearson do battle with *us*? When will Josh T. Pearson wipe *us* from the face of the earth?

Day three. 'Are you going religious?', says Sal. 'I hate it when you go religious'. We're having a religious afternoon, we tell her, as we sip our beers in the sun. God's here, we tell her. God's everywhere, we tell her. But this only winds her up.

'You don't even believe in God!' We do when we drink, we tell her. We drink to find God, we tell her, well, the Messiah, we tell her. And when we wake up, hungover, we know we've lost it again: messianism, the messianic epoch.

Everyone's religious nowadays, we tell her. Look at the kids! We look around us at the other festival-goers. The men have long beards, the women have long hair. They look peaceful, serene, sipping their beers in the sun. It's like a revivalist meeting, we agree. Ah, this is what it will be like after the revolution!

The last day, queuing for the bus.

You have to be gentle with the young, W. says. They're a gentle generation, like fauns, he says, and require a special tenderness. Their lives are going to be bad — very bad — and, at the very least, we should be tender with them, and not remind them of what is to come.

Our generation, he says, still had hope. The residues of hope. Theirs has nothing; hope itself is a luxury. What chance do they have?, W. says.

They don't want much, W. says. They don't expect a great deal. As for us . . . We come from the last of the generations that looked for a great change, for a kind of revolution to occur, W. says. —'And it might have happened, too', he says. Didn't Godard make a film on W.'s university campus?

True, that was long before he arrived. But there were still communists outside the student union in his time. It seemed like the *beginning* of times rather than the end of them, the endless end, W. says.

Hindu pathos is very mysterious to the Jew, W. says. Why, for example, did I send W. the creation hymn from the Vedas?

> *There was neither non-existence nor existence then; there was neither the realm of space nor the sky which is beyond. What stirred? Where? In whose protection? Was there water, bottomlessly deep? Was there death or immortality? Was there a sign of night and day? Who really knows?*
>
> *Who will here proclaim it? Whence was it produced? Whence is this creation? The gods came afterwards, with the creation of this universe. Who then knows whence it has arisen? Perhaps it formed itself, or perhaps it did not. Only the one who looks down on it, in the highest heaven, only he knows — or perhaps he does not know.*

Where the Hindu finds pathos, W. says, the Jew finds only evasion and vagueness.

In the depths of the night, lying awake while the world is asleep, W. asks himself the great questions. How did it all begin? Why is there something rather than nothing? Why is there anything at all? It's the *fact of existence* that confounds him, as it has confounded so many philosophers.

But above all, it is the fact of *my* existence that confounds him, and that confounds him alone. Why? How? Who put me here? Who's responsible? Was it a joke? A kind of cosmic trial? And why was I placed before *him*? This is the question, the question of questions, W. says.

It's time, W. says. No: it's after time. It's too late. We're living a posthumous life.

Perhaps this is already hell, W. muses. Perhaps we already live in hell — is that it? They — the ones we once were — lived out their whole lives somewhere else. No doubt they committed terrible crimes. No doubt they were guilty of the worst. And we're what's left, serving out our sentence having been stripped of our memories . . . Hell, but perhaps it's heaven, for is life really so bad? Not now, not today, on this pleasant afternoon . . .

Or perhaps, W. muses, we're souls waiting to be reborn. Perhaps this is a great waiting room; this, the time before a dentist's appointment, when nothing very important happens: we leaf through a magazine, we gaze out of the window . . .

But they've forgotten to call our names, haven't they? They've forgotten we are here, in the eternal waiting room. We've been left to ourselves, like abandoned children. And our seriousness is only a sham seriousness; our apocalypticism is only a kind of dressing up; and all our books, all our philosophies, are only articles in some gossip magazine . . .

The '80s are coming back, we agree with the taxi driver as we pull out of Liverpool Station. The crash is coming. Hasn't our financial friend told us that? It'll destroy Liverpool! W. lived in Liverpool in the '80s, he says. He remembers what it was like. And to think it's going to happen again! My God, what they did to Liverpool! My God, what they're going to do to it!

This is the city of *Anglican Cathedral*, W. wants to tell them. —'Have you seen *Saint James's Cemetery*?', he wants to say. But to them, the wreckers of civilisation, there are no such things as cities. To them, there are only nodes in the global network, only arbitrary nexuses of resources. This is the city of *The Philharmonic* pub, W. wants to say. This is the city of the *urinals* of *The Philharmonic* pub. But capitalism does not listen.

W. feels like the boy in Tarkovsky's *Mirror* who cannot follow orders. Turn around!, he and the other cadets are told. He turns only half the way round, 180 degrees, ending up faced in the opposite direction to his fellow cadets. —'Why can't you follow orders?', he's asked. —'You told me to turn!', he says. And then, 'I don't understand', he says. His parents died in the Siege of Leningrad, another cadet says, off camera.

His parents are dead. He's turned right round. Later, we see him walking along, whistling. Whistling and weeping. That's what W. will be doing, he says, walking along like a dazed ox, and whistling, tears running down his face . . . —'I don't understand', that's all he will say. It's all he will be able to say . . .

Steel shutters pulled down over shopfronts. Smashed glass and rubbish in the wind. Towns abandoned. Cities. Great walls raised against the world, to keep the migrants out (the rest of the world scorched, baked black . . .)

Then methane will come steaming up from melting permafrost. Then it will come bubbling up from the ocean floor. Then the Arctic ice will melt away. Then the seas will turn to acid. Then the skies will turn black. Then the lights will go out, and there'll be darkness everywhere. We'll die lingering deaths. We'll die in the sludge, very slowly.

'I don't understand', that's what W. will be saying, face down in the sludge. 'I don't understand'.

The suburbs of Liverpool. Up early, we step out into the sun, out to find a café. Another day, full of possibilities! . . . —'Which we will crush', says W.

'Have you had any thoughts yet?', W. asks me. None, I tell him. —'It's like Zen', says W. 'Pure absence'.

I should work more, W. tells me. An hour a day, that's all he asks. If I can't work at home, then I should work in the office. And if I can't work in the office, then I should find a café. And if I can't find a café, then a bench in the open air, next to the alcoholics. And if I can't find a bench? —'Then lie on the road and let the cars run over you'.

One day, W. says, and this is his hope, his hope against hope, I'm going to surprise everyone with my salmon-leap. One day, catching everyone unawares, there will be my great leap upstream — my leap, flashing the light back from my scales, my sunshine-touched leap against the current of my own idiocy: that's what he believes, somehow or other. He still believes it, still sees it above the foaming water. Up and forming a great flashing arc . . .

And where will I be going? In the *opposite direction* to my dissoluteness and squalor. In the *opposite direction* to my compromise and half-measures. And where will he be—he, W.? Leaping with me, he says. Leaping, his arching inter-linked with my own.

'You're less and less able to listen to the presentations of others', W. says. He can see it on my face. —'You can't hide it'. At one point, he says, I might as well have been lying on the floor and moaning.

What am I thinking about?, he wonders. But he knows full well. The expanses of nature. Open stretches of water. Don't I always demand, in the midst of presentations, to be taken to an *open stretch of water*?

There was the lake at Titisee, where we hired a pedallo, W. remembers. There was the trip to the river Ill, when I fully intended to strip down and swim, he says. Then there was our aborted Tamar trip, our boating expedition to the naval dockyards . . . How disappointed I had been!

Yes, he sees it in me, in one who has no feel for nature at other times. He sees it: a desperate yearning for those expanses that are as empty as my head and across which gust the winds of pure idiocy.

The Mersey Estuary at sunset. The water is red; the other shore, blue. It's like being at the end of the world, we agree. Or the beginning.

'Rivers are sacred to Hindus, aren't they?', W. says. All rivers are the Ganges to the Hindu, he knows that. All rivers flow from Shiva's matted locks as he meditates, eyes closed, in the Himalayas, and all rivers flow into the same sea.

The same sea: W. thinks of Plymouth Sound, where the rivers Plym and Tamar come together. *The same source*: W. thinks of Dartmoor, looming behind his city. Dartmoor is Plymouth's equivalent of the Himalayas, just as the Cheviots, which I pointed out to him blue and ghostly in the distance from the top of the hill on the Town Moor, are Newcastle's equivalent of the Himalayas.

The Himalayas: that's where Shiva caught the goddess-river when she fell from heaven . . . And that's where he retreated to meditate when his goddess-wife gave herself up in sacrifice. Will I head to the hill on the Town Moor when I've sacrificed him?, W. wonders. Will I ascend to commune with my strange gods?

Every year, local Hindus lower an icon of Ganesha into the Mersey, we read in our tourist books. It's carried by the tide into the open waters, and borne out along the estuary to the sea. That's where I'm sending him, W. says, he knows that: out to sea. There's where we're both heading: into the blue distance . . .

Liverpool, port of the slave trade, W. muses. —'*This has been one of the darkest places on the earth* . . . ' Liverpool, the seat of empire, the seat of conquest . . .

W. feels like Conrad's Marlowe, he says, beginning his great story about the heart of darkness, in a boat marooned in an estuary somewhere.

My trip overseas. My period as a *world traveller*. It's W.'s favourite story, he says, as we look across the Mersey. I'd flown off to the Mediterranean, hadn't I?, W. says. I'd flown there as a *world traveller*, never to return to the suburbs! Did I speak the language? Had I made preparations for my visit? Did I know anything about the culture and mores of the country I was going to? The answer is *no* in each case, W. says. I just went, didn't I? Off I went as a *world traveller*.

What did I expect? What did I think awaited me there? That I'd be recognised for what I was, at last? That the Mediterranean world would carry me off on its shoulders? Was that what I was dreaming of, W. asks, with my plans for *world travel*? Is that what I thought awaited me on the other side?

And instead, what happened? I lurched from disaster to disaster, didn't I? No sooner was I off the plane than I was beaten down by the sun—beaten by it. I'd never experienced Mediterranean heat before, had I? I'd never seen a cloudless sky. And that blue—the fierce blue of a sky without clouds. It was too much for me, wasn't it?

I became curiously mute. I'd been stunned into silence. I didn't say a thing. What could I say? What could I have said? Nothing was going to happen to me. I'd be picked up and carried along on the shoulders of no crowd. There was no one to whom I could prove myself.

Who was interested in me? Who knew my name? If I was a little younger, a paedophile might have followed me around. A little younger, a little cuter, and some pervert with a camera might have taken pictures. But then, there, in the Mediterranean heat, no one wanted to know me. No one spoke to me, not even from pity.

Because I had the wrong personality, didn't I? The entirely wrong personality. I was not a *world traveller*. I was not a go-getter. I was not a hail-fellow-well-met kind of person. I was surly, as I am now. I was churlish. I kept to myself—who would have wanted to know me? I spoke to no one—who would have wanted to listen?

What had the Mediterranean to do with me?—that was my thought, wasn't it? What had it to do with me, with its remorseless sky, its heat, its beaches, its sunbathers? And what was I to it—an idiot with a rucksack and a head full of daft ideas? Where did the circles intersect: the set of the Mediterranean and the set of Lars?

I slept rough, didn't I? I slept in a building site and then out in the open, on the rocks, the strap of my rucksack around my arm for security. I slept on a beach, didn't I, and the sea came up? I thought: *I'll sleep on this beach, how romantic!*, and then the sea came up and soaked my rucksack. The waves came in and I had to flee, didn't I, *world traveller*? Up they came, the waves, and off I went into town, towards God-knows-where in the darkness, because I was lost, hopelessly lost on a Mediterranean island.

Why had I travelled to that island in the first place? Why did I book a ticket there, to that island, among all the others? It was something about the Book of Revelations, wasn't it? It had been written there, hadn't it? Did I think some great vision was going to befall me? Did I think I'd see the end of the world? What did I see on the beach, as the waves came up? What, as I was driven into town, looking for somewhere sensible to stay?

How long did I last out there in the Mediterranean? How long, in my new life as a *world traveller*? A few days, that was it, wasn't it? A few days — a handful — instead of a lifetime. And there it was, green England, I could see it from my plane window. Green England — lush, verdant — and not the rocky Mediterranean.

Had I had any visions?, W. says, rocking back and forth with laughter. Had I finished a new Book of Revelations? Had something of the apocalypse been revealed to me? Ah, it's his favourite story, W. says.

A Book of Revelations: was that what I was going to write?, says W. in a bar on the Liverpool quayside. A new Book of Revelations, a new Apocalypse of John: is that why I journeyed out to the Greek islands? It's the funniest thing of all, W. says, the thought of me heading out on the ferry from Piraeus to Patmos with my *divine mission* in mind. Hilarious! What did I intend to do? What did I think would happen?

Of course Piraeus is disgusting now, everyone knows that. Was it really where I was going to begin my mystical journey? I must have been disappointed, W. says. I was, wasn't I? Athens was bad enough, that's what I told him, but Piraeus! Piraeus was an abomination! But I was borne along in a dream. I had my dream. I drifted along, a young idiot, a young fool.

'And what did you have in your rucksack?', W. asks. 'What was in there?' He pauses dramatically. 'Your *typewriter!*', exclaims W. 'Your typewriter . . . ' It was some time ago, W. says. Before laptops, at any rate. Well, before they became cheap. And a pen and paper wouldn't do, would it? Not for receiving the new Revelation of John. Not for taking dictation apropos the apocalypse. A typewriter! A typewriter was essential! It's hilarious, W. says. How much did it weigh?

'There you were', says W., 'on the ferry with your rucksack and your typewriter'. What books did I bring? Did I take anything to read? Oh he forgot, W. says. I was going to give up reading, wasn't I? I was going to let it go. Books were going to drop out of my hand . . . What was I going to do instead? Act? Step into the world? —'Hilarious!', W. says. 'The temerity!', he says. Write? Yes, that was it, wasn't it?, he says. I was going to write. To write a new Book of Revelations.

'Of course, you never got to your island, did you?' It had gone wrong at Piraeus. I'd asked for the *wrong island*, or they misheard me, or they wanted to misdirect me. But I was heading for *Paros*, not *Patmos*. *Paros*, and by mistake — the party island! That was my *mystical journey*, W. says. A trip to a party island!

'What did you think as the ferry docked? *Patmos has become ever so commercial* — is that what you thought? *It's very noisy on Patmos* — was that it? *People don't wear much on Patmos* — was that it?'

Still, I made good, didn't I? I slept on a rock and woke in the sun. It was Sunday. Old ladies poured pomegranate seeds into my cupped hands. And then, rucksack on my back, up I went to the deserted monastery. I sat in the shade by the spring, didn't I? I washed my face in the spring, lit a candle in the chapel, and rested, waiting for inspiration.

Imagine it: a Hindu in a Greek Orthodox monastery, completely deserted. A Hindu ready to write a new Book of Revelations. Imagine it: *Paros*, not *Patmos*! W. is on the floor, laughing. An idiot with a typewriter, on the wrong island. An idiot on his *mystical journey* . . .

'Let's look at your notebook!', says W. He's sure something important must be written there. He's sure that's where he'll find the answer.

> *And now it comes, the point of all points, which the Lord has truly revealed to me in my sleep: the point of all points for which there*

Those were Rosenzweig's last words, says W. That's what he spelled out on his letterboard, blink by blink, when he was totally paralysed. He didn't finish, says W. He wasn't able to.

What would he, W., spell out if he were paralysed? Slowly, with the greatest of efforts, the following letters would appear: *L-A-R-S--I-S--A--C-O-C-K*.

Kafka's last words were a different thing entirely, W. says. He wrote on scraps of paper because he couldn't speak. *A bird was in the room*, that was one of them. *Lemonade. Everything was so infinite*, that was another. Whatever did he mean?

Brod saved Kafka's conversation slips, W. says, as perhaps

he, W., should save my notes. 'Give me your notebook!', cries
W. 'Give it to posterity'.

'*Beard of fat*', W. reads from its pages. There's an illus-
tration, too. —'Did you draw this?' A picture of a belly, or
a stomach, and of some grey stuff hanging off the belly. Of
course, it was W. who told me about the beard of fat. Fat
does not *accumulate* in the stomach so much as *hang off* it
like a beard, he told me. —'That's what makes your belly
round', he said.

'*Bickering*', W. reads out. He remembers how Sal and I
bickered in America. —'The British working class in action',
W. explained to our hosts.

'*Stretches of water*', W. reads. A crude picture of a boat
on the waves. —'You must have been very bored', W. says.
He knows I dream of great stretches of water when I'm bored.
Hadn't I demanded to be taken to the Mersey when we were
in Liverpool? And what about the lake at Titisee when we
were in Freiburg?

W. comes to my poems, the ones I read to him when I'm
drunk.

*The wrong venue / the wrong city / the wrong time /
the wrong conference / We are the wrong people /
We are wrong*

It has a marvellous simplicity, he says. And it's so true.
Another:

*Why do we fail at the level of the banal / It's not
about thought, or whether we can think / but about
not being able to have a shit / or being locked out of
our bedrooms*

That's more like an aphorism than a poem, W. says.
And then,

*General incompetence is what will defeat capitalism /
that's why our general incompetence should make us
laugh / even though it makes us cry*

Very deep, W. says. There are several drawings too.
—'They're from your David Shrigley phase, aren't they?'
And something W. himself wrote: '*Your sin is the pun-
ishment of my life*'. When did he write that?, W. wonders.
Sounds about right, though.

On the train, leaving Liverpool. Luckily, the bar sells Plymouth Gin. We pour our little bottles into plastic cups and toast our stupidity, as the rain runs diagonally down the windows.

W.'s hair is piled up in a great quiff. Does he pomade his hair?, I ask. No, he says, it's naturally like that. What is pomade, anyway? He's got no idea, he says.

W. looks like Gary Glitter, post-disgrace, I tell him. I look like a thug, W. says. A monkey thug with great dangling arms. —'Who could suspect you of any *delicacy of thought?*', W. says. 'You look like what you are. You can't pretend otherwise'. What about him, then? Was Gary Glitter a philosopher? Did Solomon Maimon have a quiff?

I should grow my hair, W. says. He's always said that. He's never liked my suedehead. But at least I've stopped wearing vests. W.'s seen the bags of vests in my flat, he says. Primark vests in military green, which cost no more than two pounds each, made by some third world child. It's a scandal, he says.

You should never try and buy your own clothes, W. learned that long ago, he says. Sal buys his clothes for him, which is why he looks so natty.

'You need a woman in your life', W. says. 'No woman

would have permitted your *vest phase*'. And then, 'Your *vest phase*', W. says, and shudders. —'What were you thinking?' And then, 'It's not as if you have a body worth showing off. You're fat, not muscly. And you're pale, you have that dreadful northern European pallor, for all your Hindu genes'.

The Dane in me is always ascendant, W. says. I'm Scando-trash, I can't help it.

W. wants to nap, he says, but he knows I won't let him. He slouches down in his seat, moaning softly. He wants to nap now so he can be up early tomorrow. He has to work. He's got reading to do!, he says, but he knows this won't sway me.

If he's quiet for a moment, W. says, I'll start sharing my ideas with him, my mad ideas, which he would never usually give me a chance to share. He's weak, he says, he's at his lowest, but the last thing he wants to hear are my *caffeine theories*, or my musings on the way I will be sacked.

I've never been able to sleep, W. knows that. I can never get a full night's rest, and this is no surprise. I'm up all night, wandering from bedroom to bathroom, eternally disturbed by my own digestive system, eternally awoken and reawoken.

Something inside me won't allow me to sleep, W. says. There's something unsettled, some debt that has to be paid. I'm my own ghost; I haunt myself, looking for some kind of retribution, something that might *bring it all to an end*, though it will never end.

That's my insomnia, W. says: the endlessness of my guilt. Nothing can end, W. says, and nothing can really begin for me, either. Every day, the same failure. Every night, the same punishment.

'How many times do you get up at night? Ten times? Twenty?' He's never experienced anything like it, W. says. He hears me when he visits for the weekend. He's half-asleep in the living room on the blow-up mattress, and there am I, wandering up and down the hall in my vest. Up and down, up and down . . .

It doesn't wake him up as such, W. says. He would barely remember my eternal trudging, the eternal flushing of the toilet, if it did not accord with the restlessness *he* feels between the walls of my flat. He wouldn't wake up at all, W. says, if it weren't for *his* disturbed stomach, which only happens when he visits me, if it weren't for *his* insomnia, unknown to him except within the walls of my flat.

Ah, how many times has he sat up bleary-eyed in the morning, as I clear a space amidst the half-finished wine bottles and empty cheese packets to make us coffee? How many mornings has he tried to tell me of the horrors he has undergone, as I brush plaster dust from my dressing gown, and prepare our breakfast?

You have to have a balanced life to have the right perspective on things, W. says. You have to have things in order. What perspective can I possibly have from my flat, which is to say, my pit underground? What valid judgement can I make about the world, given that I spend so much time *below pavement level*?

I'm always *looking up* at things, W. says; I have to. I *look up* to see the plants and the algae in my disgusting yard. I *look up* to the concrete and the rotting bricks. I barely know the sky exists, W. says — and the sun: when was the last time I saw the sun?

Only the rats are below you, W. says. Only the rats can you look down upon.

No, the flat is not a place from which I can be expected to make any kind of valid judgement. It's set my thoughts askew, permanently askew. I can only have *damp thoughts* and *murine thoughts*. I can only have thoughts that unconsciously *look up* to what they might have been if they were thought by a strong and vigorous thinker.

What will happen the next day — the day after we destroy ourselves?, W. wonders. A holy silence. Birds singing. A great sigh will go up from the whole of creation. Have I ever felt, as he has, that the world is waiting for us to disappear, that the knot will be untied, the damage undone? Meanwhile, our lives. In the meantime, our friendship, which is really the *destruction* of friendship.

Something has gone very badly wrong, W. can't avoid that conclusion. And in some important way, it's all our fault. W. holds us responsible, he's not sure why. But what would I know of this? How could I understand the *depths* of the disaster? It's my idiocy that protects me, W. says. It burns above me like a halo.

'If you knew, if you really knew' . . . but I don't know, says W. I have intimations, to be sure. I have a sense of the disaster, but no more than that. Only he knows, W. says. Only he, of the pair of us, knows what will happen.

A series of jerks and tics, like those of a hanged man in his final death throes; a series of involuntary and grotesque spasms: that will have been my life, W. says.

It's not even desperation; it's more basic than that. There's a rebellion at the level of my *bare existence*, W. says. —'You shouldn't exist. You should never have been born': that's what my body knows. It's what *I* know at some abysmal level. And meanwhile, there I am twitching over the void, a man half-hung, neck broken . . .

My decline is precipitous, W. says. It seems to be increasing, he says. And like a cyclone of stupidity, I seem to be gathering everything up as I pass, him included, his whole life, W. says.

How could I understand what I've unleashed?, W. wonders. Does the storm understand that it is a storm? Does the earthquake know that it is an earthquake? I will never understand, says W.; that's my always appealing innocence.

It's time for the reckoning, W. says. It's reached that point. But with whom can he reckon? How to tackle an enemy who has no idea he's an enemy?

We ought to be content to write ragged books, W. says on the phone. Ragged books for a ragged world. Oh, he forgot, W. says. I already do.

W.'s learning ancient Greek for his new book, he says. It's going to be on religion. He was going to do a book on *time*, but he's decided against that. Religion, he says, that's his topic, and for that he needs Greek. And maths! If he's going to write about Cohen and God, as he intends to, he'll have to understand the infinitesimal calculus.

He's reading *The Logic of Pure Knowledge*, W. says. In German! It's taken him a year so far, and he's only on page 50. He sends me his notes:

Leibniz: the differential. The ground of the finite is the infinitely small. It is the infinite that founds the finite, and not the finite the infinite — this is why the infinite is not a negative concept.

Don't I see?, W. says, with great excitement. The infinite founds the finite. The infinite is not a negative concept, according to Cohen, W. says. It is an *originary positivity*, prior to both affirmation and negation. The infinite is the *condition* of the finite, and not the other way round, W. says.

Of course, it's all in Aristotle, W. says. *Indefinite* judgement, that's what Aristotle calls it. *Infinite* judgement: that's what Boethius called it, in his commentary on Aristotle. But it's all lost in Kant, that's what Cohen shows, W. says. Kant collapses the difference between kinds of privative judgement. But Cohen remembers!, W. says. Cohen knows!

Ah, but what would I understand of any of this?, W. says.

In a way, W. learned about originary positivity from me, he says. From my example. I've taught him a lot, despite myself. In a strange way, he's been *my* student, *my* protégé.

He was inspired to follow my example the other night, W. says. —'Oh, it was nothing to do with your *thought*'. What then? He bought a bottle of wine and went home and drank it all. Then he got beneath his bed covers and moaned. —'Oh, my troubles! Oh, my life! They're out to get me! I'm going to be next!' —'That's how you live, isn't it?'

And shouldn't I inspire others, too? W. would like to exhibit me, he says. He'd like to put me on display before a learned society as a living example.

'Don't you see?', W. would tell our audience, pointing at me with his stick. 'Isn't it clear?' 'Think!', he would command, and I would exhibit my *non*-thinking. 'Pray', he would command, I would exhibit my *non*-religiosity. 'Dance!', he would command, and I would exhibit my *non*-dancing, my chicken dancing, and our audience would gasp in awe and horror . . .

We're dead men, W. says, the walking dead. Oh God, the burden of disgust, of absolute disgust! We're disgusted with ourselves, we'll tell anyone who asks us. We've become terrible bores, speaking only of our disgust and our self-disgust.

Exiled and wretched, Solomon Maimon — the ever-neglected Maimon — is said to have given accounts of his disgrace for the price of a drink. And us? Who will listen to the story of *our* disgrace? *We* will have to buy *them* drinks, that's the terrible thing, W. says. *We* will have to pay *them* to listen to *us*. Even our disgrace is uninteresting.

Adam, says the Talmud, was originally made a golem; only afterwards did God give him *human* life. The latter is an act no human creator can imitate, says W., but the former — merely animating shapeless clay — lies in the power of the great rabbis.

Perhaps I am *his* golem, W. says. Perhaps he conjured me up from a sense of his own failure. Perhaps I am only the *way* in which W. is in the wrong, the incessant embodiment of his error.

Martinis at the *Plymouth Gin Cocktail Bar*. This is the way to spend Saturday afternoon, W. says.

His entrance key to the cocktail bar is his proudest possession. Only the most select Plymouthians are given one, he says. Only those people the bar staff *personally like*.

It's an especial honour to one, like W., who is not a *native son* of the city, W. says. It means the Plymouthians regard him as one of their own.

'Do you think the Geordies regard you as one of *their* own?', W. says. Do they see me as a *man of the toon*? He remembers our afternoon in *The Crown Pasada*, when W. fell into *football conversation* with the people at the next table.

I was silent, as usual, W. says. I said nothing. My inability to talk about football is a major flaw, W. says. My inability to talk about *anything*. —'Do you consider yourself a man of conversational range?', W. asks. 'What *can* you talk about? What topics do you feel comfortable with? Go on, say something interesting'.

I begin to tell him about my troubles at work, but W. stops me. He's heard it all before, he says. Too many times! And besides, W.'s work troubles are much greater than mine.

I begin to talk of my *romantic* troubles, but W. says he's heard too much about them, too. —'You bring them on yourself'.

I begin to tell him about my general *life* troubles, but W.'s never really believed that I am genuinely troubled, he says. I'm a petty man, yes; a troubled man, no. A man who wails and moans at the slightest thing: obviously; a man who knows the meaning of suffering: obviously not.

I begin to tell him of the troubles of my past. This is potentially interesting, W. says. He likes to stare with me into the *plague pit of my memories*. Sometimes he thinks of me as a kind of *martyr*—to what, he doesn't know.

Anyway, I'm boring him now, W. says, and reads out a passage from Rosenzweig:

> *Nature and revelation: the same material, but opposite ways of being exposed to the light. The more everyday the material, the more revealing and revealed can it become.*

Religion is only ever about the everyday, W. says with great firmness. That's what Rosenzweig saw in rejecting mysticism. Revelation is a public affair! It's about ritual, about ceremony as it is lived between people. And above all, it is about *speech*.

That's why Rosenzweig abandoned academia, W. says. He was looking for another kind of speech. He was looking to be interrupted. Henceforward, he vowed only to inquire when he found himself *inquired of*, that's what he said. And inquired of by *people, ordinary people* rather than scholars.

Ah, have we ever been *inquired of?*, W. says. Would we know what it meant? —'Interrupt me!', he cries. 'Go on, say something!' But he knows I'll only arse about, he says. He knows I'll make the wrong kind of interruption.

Smashed glass on the cobblestones, vomit on the Mayflower Steps: Plymouth quayside, Saturday night.

We're among the people, W. says as we drink our pints of Bass in *The Dolphin*. We're in the midst of everyday life. Didn't Rosenzweig say that *theological problems must be translated into everyday terms, and everyday problems brought into the pale of theology?*, W. says. Didn't he say that *philosophical problems must be translated into those of everyday life, and everyday life brought into the pale of philosophy?*

Rosenzweig's task is our task, we agree, looking round the bar. This is where philosophy must begin anew, right here in the pub! This is where theology will be reborn, in the thick of the everyday!

'My God, they were so drunk, weren't they?', W. says in the taxi on the way home. *We* were drunk, I tell him. We *are* drunk. What were we talking about?, W. wonders. Did he really give an impromptu sermon on the apocalypse, on the end of times? He remembers the merchant seamen nodding their heads. The miserable record of Plymouth Argyll FC, W. told them; the threat of the Royal Navy to withdraw from the city; the colonisation of Plymouth by students: all signs of the apocalypse, W. said. Signs of the End of Times, they all agreed.

The working class know that the end is coming, W. says. They can sense it. And perhaps they have a sense of the messianic, too; W.'s not sure. But we *spoke*, that was the main thing. We spoke to strangers. Was that what it means to be *inquired of*?

Speech, speech. Will we ever understand what is meant by this word? The *old thinking*, as Rosenzweig calls it, is content with abstraction, says W. The *old thinker* is alone, alone before the timeless. But the *new thinking* depends upon speech, which is bound to time and nourished by it. The *new thinker* neither can nor wants to abandon this element, that's what Rosenzweig thinks, according to W.

Ah, but what does the Hindu understand of speech, of the significance of speech?, W. says. One doesn't have to understand the meaning of the Vedic mantras for them to do their work, haven't I told him that? It's enough just to hear them, an indecipherable murmuring, which is why they pipe them over loudspeakers in Indian hotels. It's good luck just to be in their presence, W. says. But this means that the Hindu is never *inquired of*, he says. The Hindu is never *interrupted*.

Our *twelfth* Dogma presentation . . . what can we recall of that? What really happened? W.'s unsure; I'm unsure. Was there shouting? Were we forcibly ejected from the auditorium? Was there a diplomatic incident? Did I expose myself? Did W.? Did *I* expose *him*? Something happened, we're sure of that, but we have only screen memories of the whole fiasco. We remember only owls, swooping through the night.

And the *thirteenth*? We skipped the *thirteenth* presentation altogether. W. was always superstitious, he says.

For the *fourteenth*, W. spoke of my shortcomings, I of his. He cursed me and I cursed him. We came to blows. It was a performance piece, we agreed. It was a *gestural* form of Dogma.

The *fifteenth*, the notorious *fifteenth,* was for our benefit only. We gave it in secret, under cover. No one must know! That's what we said to ourselves. Dogma has to undergo a profound occultation. We had to draw it back to the source. To draw ourselves back! It was like a sweat lodge, we remember.

And the *sixteenth*? It was in the great outdoors, we remember. On one of our walks over Jennycliff to Bovissands. I held forth for over an hour, W. remembers, visibly moved. The clouds parted. All of nature paused to listen. But I spoke only to myself, W. says. My presentation was inaudible to him. —'You muttered. You murmured'. I was like a druid, W. says. It was as though I commanded great forces, and was casting a spell.

His presentation was much more sober, W. remembers. It had to be; I needed a counterbalance. He berated and harangued me. He listed my faults, and my many betrayals of him. It took a long time; nearly all the way back to the city. He was still speaking as we crossed the bay in the water taxi, concluding only when we reached *Platters*.

The *seventeenth*? We don't want to remember the *seventeenth*. It was a misstep, W. says. It was misconceived from the first. We're not dancers, and we should never try to be. Of course, we were trying to dance as *non-dancers*, but who would know that?

The *eighteenth* was to be an action presentation. It was to be Dogma's first murder. But we got scared and backed out. It was not yet time for the *Dogma Terror*.

'*We are nihilistic thoughts, suicidal thoughts that come into God's head*: that's Kafka', W. says. So God, too, wants to die?, he wonders. It's not just us?

Death, death: W. hears the great bells tolling in the sky. We're at the end, the very end! There can't be much more, can there? This is it, isn't it? The credits are rolling . . . The game is up . . .

They're calling him home, W. says. He sees them as figures filled and flooded with light, the philosophers of the past, the other thinkers. Is that Kant? Is that Schleiermacher? Is that Maimon, made of light?

And meanwhile, what's happening to me? I'm falling, W. says. I'm heading down, only down, W. says. And who do I see? Is that Sabbatai Zevi, the apostate Messiah? Is that Alcibiades, the betrayer of Athens? Is that the *humanzee*, bred in Soviet research labs?

The rats are dying, I tell W. on the phone. I can hear them squeaking, which they only do when they're distressed—that's what the pest controller said. I hear them squeaking at night in agony.

Oh God, the smell! I say to W. on the phone, a week later. It's so thick, so pungent. It's almost *sweet*, I tell him. The flat smells of a kind of sweet rotting. Is this what death smells like? Is this what it smells like at the end?

A week later. There's been a plague of *bluebottles* in the flat, I tell W. They're coming up from beneath the floorboards, I tell him. They must be hatching in the darkness beneath the flat. They're huge! They buzz against the window in small swarms, I never know how many there are. And that's how they die, in small swarms, their curled up bodies littering the sill.

I imagine I can hear fly eggs hatching in the darkness, I tell W. I imagine I can hear the maggots writhing. I imagine sticky sounds as I lie in the dark. I imagine the slurp of eyeless, headless maggots melting their food with enzymes. I imagine the low buzzing of bluebottles just hatched from pupae . . .

The rats will have their revenge, I tell W. I know that.

Rats always come back, the pest controller said, and they'll have learnt from their mistakes.

I think the rats are coming back in the form of flies, I tell W. I think it's flies that are going to inflict the *rat-punishment*. I can imagine a swarm of bluebottles boring through my body, I tell him. I can imagine them crawling out of my mouth . . .

Dogma: why did it chose us, the greatest of idiots?, W. wonders. Why were we singled out? It must be like the balance of electrical charges that produces lightning in clouds. There must be the greatest possible difference between positive and negative ions—and thus, with Dogma, between the highest thought and the basest idiocy. That's when lightning strikes.

But what did we *think*? What did thought set afire in us? We have no idea, no inkling. How could we? Dogma was greater than us. Dogma was broader, more generous. Weren't we only swallows in the updraft? Weren't we leaves swept up in an autumn storm?

Perhaps we didn't think anything at all: how can we know? Perhaps we simply wandered out into the snow and got lost. Perhaps it was all a dream: the last hallucinations of men dying of frostbite.

We *felt* things. That is undeniable. We set out our coracles on great currents of feeling. We had feelings; we are sure of that. Pathos opened its door to admit us. But did we *think*, too? Did thought take flight in us as feeling did? These are questions we can never answer, says W. It's for others to judge.

What did they see as our eyes rolled upward? What, as we spoke in tongues and writhed on the floor? They must have thought we were on fire, though they couldn't see the flames, says W. That we were on fire from thought: did they think that? That thought itself had set us aflame like Olympic torches?

What impression did we leave, as we exited the room? Was the light still dying in their eyes? Had they seen too much? Had they heard much too much? Did an angel with a fiery sword stand behind us?

We felt things. Like great, dumb animals, we were only feeling. We felt, like cattle lowing in the pasture. We felt, like pigs snuffling in the dirt. What could we understand of what we had been called to do?

But we were called, W.'s sure of that. We felt things. We felt the apocalypse approaching. We knew it, as animals know when an earthquake's coming. We sent up our howls into the night.

Don't you see?, we said to people. Don't you feel it?, we said, grabbing them by the lapels. We all but carried placards out into the street. *The end is nigh*: isn't that what wrote itself across every page of our essays? *Repent*: didn't that word repeat itself in everything we said?

The signs are coming faster now, we agree. The current's quickening, as it does when a river approaches the waterfall. And who are we, who can read such tell tale signs? To whom has the secret begun to reveal itself?

The apocalypse will reveal God's plan for us all, that's what it says in the Bible. And if there is no God? No plan, either.

The signs are coming faster: my life, W.'s, our friendship, our collaboration. Signs, all signs, which in turn enable us to read signs, as though our friendship was only a fold in the apocalypse, a way for it to sense its own magnitude.

W.'s been moved to a new office, now they've closed his department. His corridor's like death row, he says. It's where they put the condemned, he says. It's where they put those they are going to sack. He imagines he can hear screams from the offices adjacent to him, but when he looks out, he sees only people like himself, working at their desks.

Have they told him what he's meant to do?, I ask him. Not yet, W. says. He has no idea what they want. He's been stirring up the students, W. says. They're threatening to demonstrate against the closures. He's been stirring up the staff, too, with his impromptu speeches. But he doesn't think that it's helping his case.

What's to become of him? What's to become of *us*? Because it's no different with me, he says. —'Of what does your life consist, essentially? Where is it taking you?', W. asks. 'Where do you think it's all going?' A pause. 'Nowhere!', says W. with great vehemence. 'You're going nowhere!'

Of course, I have my constant nightmares of unemployment to spur me on, W. says. I have the job pages I read and my ridiculous fantasies about *entering management* or *beginning a new career as a lawyer*. They keep me going, W. says.

They give me the illusion of choice, when in fact I have no choice at all.

W. admires my sense of persecution. —'You really think they're out to get you, don't you? You really think you're in trouble'. I may be in trouble, W. says, but it's nothing to do with what I've done. —'It's not about you', W. says. 'It's never about you'.

When the end comes, it'll be nothing personal. —'Your name will appear on someone's list. They won't know who you are. They won't know anything about you. But they'll put a line through your name and that will be that'.

The fact that I think it's personal accounts for my desire to protest. I jump up and down like an angry ape, W. says. I hoot and wail.

One day, I'll surprise you all. One day, I'll really surprise you . . . That's what I mutter to myself in brown pub interiors, isn't it?, W. says. But drunks are full of a messianic sense of self. They're full of a sense of a great earthly mission. *Just listen for a moment*, that's what the drunk says. *Listen — just listen!*

And when W. does listen? When he gives me the floor? Nothing, he says. Silence, he says. And the great roar of my stupidity.

Dogma. What did it mean? Should we even say the word aloud? Perhaps it shouldn't be spoken of, like the name of God. Perhaps saying it only diminishes its glory, and hearing it only lessens its resonance.

Wasn't it greater than us? Broader, as the sky is broad? It was our measure. It was our ennoblement. When, otherwise, could we have been *borne* by thought, *thought* by it, rather than taking ourselves to have had thoughts of our own?

In truth, we've had no thoughts. We were ventriloquised; we spoke, but not with our own voices. We wept, but they weren't our tears. We felt things, great things, but in what sense were those feelings ours? Dogma touched us without noticing us. Dogma brushed us with its wings.

In the end, we should throw ourselves upon its shore, and ask for mercy. In the end, we should offer ourselves in sacrifice, burning upwards into the great mouth of the sky.

Dogma. What have we learnt? Have we been able, like the famous Chinese artist who vanished into his own painting, to disappear into our thought? But we had no thoughts, not really. We weren't able to think.

We *felt* things, though, didn't we? Yes, we felt things. We were moved, weren't we? Yes, we were moved. And our audience? In the end, we had no audience. We had the sea, the air. We had Plymouth Sound; we had Whitley Bay. We had our great walks and our trips by water taxi.

We had the elements, which we redeemed through our speech . . . We had each other. But did we really have that, each other?, W. wonders. Didn't we talk past each other? And didn't we also talk past ourselves? My God, we could barely understand our own words!

We felt things, to be sure. But weren't we only vessels to be smashed? Weren't we messengers to be shot? Weren't we asked to bare our chests to the bayonets? Who were we, in the end, to understand our significance?

Why can't we give up? Why press ourselves on? Why, despite everything, do we cling to life? It must be some instinct, W. says. Some residue of natural life. But then, too, our instincts have always been wrong. They've always led us in the wrong direction. We're not just *careless* of our lives, we've *wrecked* them.

W. hears the distant sound of sobbing and wonders if it's him. I hear a distant mewling, and wonder if it's me.

W.'s impressed: I'm preparing myself, he says. I know what's to come, and I've prioritised rightly. I live each day as though it were the day *after* the last. And I'm drinking my way through it. Numbing myself.

If only death would come cleanly! If only it would fall like a great axe from the sky! But that's not how it will come, and that's the horror. We won't be able to die: isn't that it? The power to die will be taken from us.

That's why we have to drink ourselves into a stupor. It's practice, practice for the coming end. That's how to meet death: dead drunk, and without a care. That's how to meet the death that will not come.

'We tried to tell them, didn't we?', says W. Yes, we tried to tell them. —'We tried to warn them?' Yes, we tried to warn them. Our lives were living warnings. We all but set ourselves on fire. We all but soiled ourselves in public. —'Actually, you did soil yourself in public, didn't you?', W. says.

No more, says W. No more. He's passing through a dead zone, he says, like the ones they are beginning to find in the oceans: blank regions where there is no life. There's no life in him! It's all over!

W.'s despairs are like magnetic fields, he says, like great clouds in the air through which he passes. They have nothing to do with his inner states at all. It's not a matter of emotion. His despairs, W. says, are not even his.

Are we even alive?, asks W. Is this even happening? Are we really talking — right now? Because all he can hear is a great roaring, W. says. He's falling, W. says, as through the clouds of Jupiter.

When will he ever hit anything real? When will he strike

his head upon the hard shore of the real? Because that's what he wants, even if it dashes his head to pieces. That's all he wants, and especially if it dashes his head to pieces . . .

Only death is real, W. says, and it's time to die. But death isn't coming any closer. If anything, he's *too* healthy, and so am I. We need to be struck down, eradicated, along with everyone who has known us. Our memory should be wiped from the earth . . .

Sometimes W. finds the coming disaster a comforting thought. It will be a relief, a blessed relief, the parched earth, the boiling sky. Because won't it entail *our* annihilation? Won't it mean, at the very least, *our* complete destruction?

Only the disaster is real, W. says. There is no future. And isn't that a relief: that there is no future? And meanwhile, his long fall. Meanwhile our long fall through the clouds . . .

Our eternal puppet show, says W. Our endless ventriloquy. Who's speaking through us? Who's using our voices? Sometimes he swears he hears a voice within our own, W. says. He can hear it, he says, on the threshold of audibility, a little like the grinding of Pythagoras's celestial spheres. Only this time it's idiocy itself that grinds itself out. This time it's the amazing force of idiocy, a solar wind sweeping through empty space.

Where's it all going? Where's it all leading? Is there a pattern? Is the pattern falling apart? W.'s in the dark, and it's not a propitious darkness. It is not a resting place. There are terrible stirrings out there. Murmurs.

Something is awakening. Something is turning in its sleep. And as it turns, we turn too. Will our lives make sense one day, when it wakes? Will it all become clear on the day another part of us stands and stretches in the sun?

It's come. It's finally happened. He's being made redundant. They're running him out of the college on a rail, W. says. Even I, with my *Hindu fatalism*, couldn't have predicted this.

He's been banned from teaching, W. says. They've threatened to escort him from the premises, if he engages in any more 'seditious behaviour' . . . But he's never engaged in seditious behaviour, W. says. He's only ever *told the truth*.

What's worse is that no one wants to see him, W. says. No one wants to see a *dead man walking*, W. says. It would remind them of their shame and their lies. It would remind them of the horror of their moral compromise, which even they can feel.

They can't bear to look at him, W. says. They retreat into doorways as he approaches. They turn away from him. Because he is a dead man walking and it's all their fault, he says. Because his life has been ruined and it's all their doing.

He had been waiting for the end, W. says, and still the end surprised him. That's the lesson, he says: the end will always come too soon. The end will be there, tapping on the window . . .

They'll put a sack on your head. They'll lead you through the forest. They'll make you kneel . . . Will you cry out for mercy? Will you accept your fate solemnly, with dignity? Or will you piss and shit yourself in fear? Will you make a run for it, before braining yourself on a tree?

For what cause are you dying? You don't know. You'll never understand. It's beyond you, your role in all this. What is certain is that you must die. Your time has come. You thought you had years — decades — but your time has passed, you've outlived your time, this is it . . .

W. is making a run for it, he says, sack on head. Any moment now, he'll brain himself on a tree . . .

W.'s seeking my help, he says. Oh, he knows I will offer him only the most grotesque parody of assistance, but that's the point. He's fully aware that I'm the last person who can help him—that bringing me along to the meeting with his employers is the most foolish of ideas.

Why not take a lawyer?, I ask him. He's allowed to. No, he wants the equivalent of an idiot child, W. says. He wants the equivalent of a diseased ape with scabs round his mouth, throwing faeces around the room.

Perhaps it will scare them. Perhaps they'll look at him in an entirely different light. Did you see who he had with him?, they'll say. *What* he had with him? My God, we shouldn't make his life any worse: that's what they'll say, W. says. And perhaps then they'll show mercy.

The kingdom of unemployment is rising to enclose him, W. says. Soon he'll be lost among the shades and spectres. Will I visit him in his new life? Will I sit with him in the gutter?

Ah, he'll finally have found the everyday, he says. He'll finally have met it at its level. He'll finally know what I know, he says. *Eternullity*, he says. *The infinite wearing away* . . .

And will he finally understand religion? Will he finally understand what God means? Will he finally utter a true word?

He knows what will happen, W. says. Gradually, he'll be forgotten. Gradually, his presence will fade from everyone's life. —'Where's W.?', they'll ask at first. But later, they will only have a sense of absence, with no knowledge of its cause. And later still, there will be no absence either. Life will be complete again, without tear. —'Even you', W. says. 'Even you will forget me'. And then, 'especially you'.

He was like a *mayfly of thought*, W. says. A single day, that's all he had. A single day—the whole of his life—in the sun.

He spread his wings, rode the thermals upwards, felt the rush of the whole landscape beneath him — all thought, all thinkers . . . And now that it's at an end? Now that his life as a thinker has passed into oblivion?

I will have to remember, W. says, that's my task. He has granted me the great task of memory, of memorialising. I'm to write the introduction to his collected works; I'm to assemble them from his extant notes, his drafts, his marginalia. I'm to leave a record of his table-talk. Because he's heading out now, onto the ice, W. says. —'I may be some time'.

'Tell me a Hindu story', W. says. 'A last Hindu story . . . '

I tell W. of the fate of Bhishma in the *Mahabharata*. This wise and virtuous man had been granted the boon of deciding the hour of his own death. There he lay, on the battlefield, his body filled with arrows.

It was time to die, white-bearded Bhishma thought. He'd lived a long life! He'd seen it all, even the disaster that was the battle on the Kurushetra plains. Even the darkness that was soon to fall over India.

The fighting around him stopped. His great-nephew, Arjuna, sought to slake his uncle's thirst by firing an arrow into the ground to let cooling spring water arc into his mouth. Silence reigned over the battlefield. And in the time that was left to him, Bhishma spoke.

He spoke of what he'd learnt in his long life. He spoke of his horror at the battle that set uncle against nephew, friend against friend. He spoke of what was to come, and his horror at what was to come. And then his white-haired head fell back, and death came as a sweetness to him.

What will *he* say, I ask W., now the end has come, the endless end? Will he speak of love? Of friendship? Of the life of thought? He'll speak about *me*, says W. Of not being able to get rid of me. Of my being here, even now . . .

It's time to die, says W. But death does not come.

LARS IYER lectures in philosophy at Newcastle University. He is the author of the novel *Spurious*, two books on Maurice Blanchot (*Blanchot's Communism: Art, Philosophy and the Political* and *Blanchot's Vigilance: Phenomenology, Literature and the Ethical*) and his blog Spurious. He is also a contributor to Britain's leading literary website, Ready Steady Book. Watch for the final book in the trilogy, *Exodus*, coming in 2013.